Based on

FULL CIRCLE

A Journey of Faith and Fly Fishing

April Conrad

Based on a True Story

FULL CIRCLE

A Journey of Faith and Fly Fishing

April Conrad

Tupelo, Mississippi

What others are saying about Full Circle

"Conventional wisdom says that first-time authors rarely get it all right. With 'Full Circle', April Conrad proves that conventional wisdom can sometimes be all wrong. Skillfully mixing a passion for fly fishing with the power of faith, Conrad takes her readers on an amazing journey that reminds us all, once again, that with God all things are indeed possible."

Chad Foster – Best-selling author and former host of ESPN's Fly Fishing America.

"This is very strong. Powerful. Moving. Inspirational. I think it's great!"

William G. Tapply – Best-selling author of *Trout Eyes, Upland Autumn, the Brady Coyne* mystery novel series and prolific writer for all things outdoors.

"It touches my heart. Conrad has a real gift for this kind of writing...Sometimes sad, sometimes scary...and beautiful. I want to jump in my car, drive home and hug my wife and son."

Tom Rosenbauer – author of the Orvis Flyfishing Guide, Reading Trout Streams, Prospecting for Trout, and many others.

"April uses unique devices in putting the story together...they are refreshing, and guarantee that the reader will read on (I did)...Well done!"

Flip Pallot – television host, and author of Mangroves, Memories and Magic, and All the Best – a biography of Lefty Kreh.

"I understand, first hand, the little divine 'nudges' April so aptly describes, and I'm struck by the epic tale of cancer and faith; hope…that is Dean's story."

R.M. Farris, MD, Chief of Staff, Scripps – Mercy Hospital.

"I was captivated after the first paragraph."

Kirk Werner – author of *Olive the Little Woolly Bugger* series.

ISBN: 978-0-9845426-0-4
Printed in the United States of America

Cover Design:
Kirk Werner, Itchy Dog Productions
www.itchydogproductions.com

Cover Art: Bob White, Whitefish Studio
www.whitefishstudio.com

Interior Formatting:
Lindsey Christian

Editorial Assistance:
Phillip Monahan
104 SE Corners Rd
Sandgate, VT 05250
802-558-6550
phil.monahan@gmail.com

Back cover photography, author photograph:
Greg Crenshaw, Crenshaw Portrait Studio, Florence, AL
www.crenshawportrait.com

Bethel Road Publications, Tupelo, MS
www.bethelroadpublications.com

Acknowledgements

I'm certain every author, upon completing their first book, struggles with how to thank the many people involved in bringing such an undertaking to fruition. I'm terrified of leaving someone out, and apologize up front for offense any omissions cause.

First and foremost, this is for my family. For my children, Anna and William, who kept Mommy's "secret project" a real secret, you kept me going and supported me; it's a blessing to have children who are enthusiastic about their parents' dreams. I hope this in some small way encourages you to always follow your own dreams. For Will, the best husband a wife ever had, who put up with late nights at the computer even when he had no idea what in the world I was working on - and because he pushed me to complete the project so I could share the finished product with him. You helped ensure this didn't just remain a pipe dream. You are my own Full Circle story. I love you.

In my opinion, every author needs their own personal cheerleading squad, and I had a bangdoodle. Sara, my prayer partner and publisher, thank you for believing in my dream and making it your own. We did it! Lori, the journey of a best friend follows some strange paths – thank you for never leaving my side. Reuben, my uncle, dad, buddy, medical consultant – you always believe in me, and helped me get it right. Brittany, you are my sanity-saver and true friend. Thanks for being as excited about this project as I was, no matter how long it took. Lynda, you are my own personal prayer warrior – you always laugh with me, never at me – what a blessing you are to my life. Rick, your spiritual guidance and friendship are invaluable. An author's success also depends on having faithful sounding boards to bounce things around with, and Kenneth and Sandy, you're awesome. Eric and Nancy, I'll recommend you as a superior 'focus group' any day of the week. John, you consistently support and encourage my crazy approaches to work-life balance. Mom, your own journey is more inspiring to me than you will ever know. I'm glad it brought us back to where we are now.

This is, after all, a book about fly fishing, and the project would not have made it this far without the advice and support from my angling friends. Many thanks to Tom, Phil, Steve, Flip and Bob. Hats off to Lefty Kreh, whose Little Library served me well. My dear friend and writing mentor, Bill Tapply, reached the end of his own journey as I finished this project. I know for certain I would have never had the guts to have started it without his direction and support, gently prodding me to follow my heart and write. Thanks to his wife, Vicki, for allowing me to share Bill's insights about the book.

Bob White, thank you for the cover art and section illustrations! You didn't brush this off as a crazy idea, and that means a lot. I'm both honored and humbled to have your amazing work grace this project. Phil Monahan, you set a high bar in the Editor department. Thank you for your guidance, patience and support. Your input made this the best it could be, and I'm forever grateful. Flip, Tom and Steve, I'll never fish all the places you've already forgotten – thanks for making the fishing real, and for your friendship. For Kirk Werner, who'd have believed you could nail a book cover on the first try? Thank you for bringing the vision to life in such an amazing way.

Don, Pam and Lindsay. You know all the reasons. You all have captured a part of my soul, and your friendship is a blessing. Thank you for sharing your lives with me.

The Bible teaches us that, "with God all things are possible." I give thanks, honor and praise for His presence along this journey with me.

For Will.

Always.

For Dad.

You introduced me to fishing,
and I'll always be grateful.
Your own journey ended
much too soon.

Many heroes lived…
but all are unknown
and unwept,
extinguished in
everlasting night,
because they have
no spirited chronicler.

Horace

Prologue

Dean Moone considered himself a pretty decent outdoorsman, having grown up camping and fishing with his family in the mountains of north Georgia. Luck had also provided many avenues for him to visit various parts of the country over the years. He and his father spent countless hours together during those early years, traipsing all over the hills and valleys in search of new fishing adventures. Sometimes his older brother Ted tagged along, but for the most part, the mountain time was Dean's time. One-on-one time with his Dad.

While pursuing their angling passions, stomping through the woods in places like Wildcat Creek and Coopers Creek, Robert Moone also introduced his son to various identification methods of flora and fauna, and sealed Dean's later appreciation of nature. For "Big Bob," as everyone called him, the experience was less about learning Latin names – though this surely was important – and more about understanding concepts like native habitat and ecosystems. By the time Dean reached the summer of his tenth year, he could tell anyone the difference between a white oak and a red oak, or even a chestnut oak, simply by its bark. He learned to look for flying squirrels, fox squirrels and rabbits, and Big Bob taught him to listen for the distinctive calls of native bird species.

Ted didn't mind hanging out with his dad and little brother. It was just more that he never connected to the fishing like Dean did, and he eventually pursued other teenage passions, while Big Bob and Dean headed to the mountains for mischief and trout.

"Was that a cardinal?" his father would ask, cupping his hand around his ear.

Dean would roll his eyes. "Daaad," he said, "you *know* that's a brown thrasher."

They both laughed, and Robert expressed his pleasure that his son could identify the song of their state bird. They quizzed each other constantly and picked on each other mercilessly, and Dean never suspected he'd succumbed to his father's subtle educational plan. He thought he was just having a ball, and into every memory a thread of fishing had been woven.

Now, back in the moment, Dean was stumped. Try as he might, he failed in his attempt to identify the multitude of birds he now heard.

Never in his thirty-eight years had he heard such a symphony coming from so many birds at once, like they had all rehearsed their songs together to be in perfect harmony and rhythm at this very moment. It hardly resembled the cacophony one imagined coming from a busy forest, with blackbirds, cardinals, mockingbirds, blue jays, and the like. He'd simply never heard anything like it—ever.

Nevertheless, he continued down the pristine path through what he would later describe as redwoods. Towering, majestic trees that seemed to sweep the clouds with their branches, protected the path with a canopy that housed the avian orchestra. Dean had no idea where he was, but realized he wasn't scared; he was more curious about what lay around the next bend.

Presently, he came to a clearing. Sunlight streamed through the branches of the giant trees, and the rays seemed to gather intensity as he neared the center of the area. By the time he stepped fully into the openness of the clearing, the light was all he could see, but for some reason it didn't hurt his eyes.

From behind the trees he could hear faint voices; he swore one belonged to his mother, and he recognized the other one as the nurse with the infectious laugh, Maxine, who took care of him after his recent bone marrow transplant. As he thought about the nurse, something about the timing suddenly didn't make sense.

Was he dreaming? Hallucinating? Were the post-op drugs playing with his mind? Dean decided on the latter—yes, it must be the drugs. He was having some sort of out-of-body trip, and wasn't sure he felt as comfortable then as he had a few moments before. As if on cue, he heard another voice. Although he'd never actually heard it in audible form, he recognized it immediately.

In almost a whisper, Dean spoke, "Okay, Lord, if this is heaven," he took a shallow breath and exhaled it in about three parts, "then I guess I'm ready."

Nothing—no reply.

"I realize this is about Your timing and Your understanding, not mine," Dean continued, "so I won't question You about it."

Silence.

He had a painful thought at that moment, however, and added quickly, "Although if I can, I'd like to make one request…to be sure my wife and daughter are okay?"

He'd not meant to make the request so timidly, but it came out in the end as more of a questioning plea. Then, Dean just waited. Should he move? Kneel? Sing? *Oh, Lord.* He put his face in his hands.

Dean, Dean—why do you worry so much?

The voice was powerful, yet at the same time the gentlest he'd ever heard.

I know you have been at peace throughout this long and agonizing journey of yours. I know that your faith remains strong, even now.

Dean was stunned. Not so much that he was in that *place*, but that he was actually having what could only be described as a conversation—with God.

"Of course, Lord," he managed to stammer out, "but, um, well, I'm embarrassed to admit…"

You're also scared.

Dean exhaled again, strongly, blowing air through tightly pursed lips. "Terrified."

Well, I would know you were lying to Me if you said you weren't scared, actually. Don't you think? But Dean, I need you to know one very important thing.

Dean froze, paralyzed. Waiting, wondering.

It's not yet your time.

Dean was shocked! He stood, in the middle of some majestic redwood forest, having a conversation with his Maker much the same as he and Sam would have over a cup of coffee at Martha's Café. And he was also trying to get his head around the fact that he was, in reality, DEAD. To be sure, the course was being changed again—and he was having trouble keeping up. Maybe it was the drugs....

He stammered, "Not my time? You mean...I get to...go ... BACK?"

That's exactly what I mean, Dean. I'm sending you back.

Though elated by this news, Dean realized he also felt a little disappointed—didn't God think he was ready for heaven? Maybe he was not supposed to be here at all? *Oh, no!* His mind rapidly flashed back over years of memories, like a movie set on fast forward; he could count dozens, no, *hundreds* of things to keep him from ever reaching this place again. He felt nauseated, and this time not from the chemo. His mind raced.

DEAN! came the voice that shook his bones like a summer southern thunderstorm. Then again, more softly, *Dean, beloved, My thoughts are not your thoughts—My ways are not your ways.*

"I've read that."

Dean, you're not meant to understand all of this. Not now. You said so yourself. You won't fully comprehend all that is happening in this moment until we meet again another time...I'm sending you back because your work for Me is unfinished.

"My work?" he answered.

Dean had taught Sunday School and participated in various local ministries over the years, but he was at a loss to understand what he was being told. He sensed more would be required of him.

Relax, child. It's not that YOU are unfinished. But I have a greater purpose for you, Dean. Please, stop with all the questions. Just chill out for a while—you'll be back soon enough, and then the rest of the purpose will reveal itself to you in time.

"Your time or my time?"

Suddenly, the light grew brighter and the leaves on the trees danced in a warm swirl of wind. Dean knew at that moment he would never forget what it felt like to feel God laugh.

Always in My time, Dean…always in My time. But also with YOUR help. People seem to forget we're meant to be on this journey together, that it really is a two-way street.

Dean stood motionless in the clearing. "What do I do now?"

Time to go. The light became gradually dimmer. He still could not move.

"Dean!" A faint yell, like someone trying to get his attention, came from beyond the clearing. "Dean!" Was it God telling him to come back? Who was it? Why were they calling him? The light grew dimmer still, then he followed his instinct, turned and ran. As he ran, he felt what he thought must be the needles from the trees scraping his chest, legs, and arms—but he couldn't see where he was going. Total darkness surrounded him.

"Dean!"

He heard beeping noises now, and not the chirps of the birds. He saw bright lights again, but not like in the clearing. These were not as bright, yet it hurt his eyes to look at them.

People repeated his name. He realized what he felt were needles and paddles shocking and pricking his body, and doctors and nurses yelled, fighting to bring him back from the forest. Their voices called to him. The lights were from the hospital room. He was back.

Bob White

Chapter 1

It is the secret of the world
that all things subsist and do not die,
but only retire from sight
and afterwards return again.

Ralph Waldo Emerson

"Doctor, we've got a rhythm," said the voice of Maxine Walker. "Steady sinus—pulse is still weak."

"BP's coming up," said another voice.

"Respiration's shallow, but he's breathing on his own," came the last.

Are they talking about me? was all he could think. Then he heard the doctor's voice again. "Well, he was gone for over nine minutes, so we'll need to wait to see if there's any permanent damage. Put in a call for the neurologist." The doctor walked out of the room, leaving the nurses and technicians to finish their work.

Tubes, electrodes, and wires sprouted from all sorts of machines connecting to Dean. He felt like a sci-fi experiment, a found alien from some foreign planet on a Star Trek voyage. But one thing was certain, he was back. Alive. And he had no doubt that what had happened when he was—well, wherever he was—was just as real as what was happening at that very moment in the hospital room.

Maxine Walker's long nursing career spanned two decades, and she'd spent that time working in oncological surgery and intensive care. Her twinkling eyes often belied her calm, professional presence; she'd never quite mastered complete objective detachment, and for that she felt blessed. Oh, it made some days quite unbearable, living through grief with families she came to care for deeply—but the reality was that it also made for some of her greatest moments of joy.

Like today. Dean Moone had been clinically dead longer than any patient Maxine had ever seen. Now she was adjusting the machines that monitored his vital signs, and they were all, for the most part, completely normal. She knew she had witnessed a miracle.

Dean tried at that moment to ask Maxine a question but found himself too weak to speak. His lips just kept making an *mmmm, mmmm* sound, so he gave up. Maxine looked at him at about the same time. Moving from the machines to his bedside, she leaned down close to him and put her hand on his shoulder.

"Praise Jesus!" she whispered in his ear. "I'm not supposed to say that real loud or too often around here, but you being back here is a *miracle*, that's just what it is. Oh, the Lord is *good*!"

Dean managed to fight through the cobwebs enough to make contact through half-opened lids. Opening his eyes seemed as difficult as prying open an oyster shell with a paperclip, and everything appeared fuzzy, out of focus; he looked up at her and then again closed his eyes. He could still see her big dark eyes, onyx saucers set in flawless skin the color of Georgia pecan shells. Her voice reminded him of his Grandy

Moone's pear preserves——thick, rich, smooth and sweet all at once, something that just made you feel good all over.

Her hand still rested on his shoulder, which she gave a gentle squeeze and then one last pat. "I can't wait to see what He has planned for you, Dean Moone! Ooh, I just can't *wait*. You rest now. I'll be back to check on you again soon."

She quietly hummed the first bars of *Amazing Grace* as she walked out of the room.

Chapter 2

When you feel like you're alone
in your sadness
and it seems like no one in
this whole world cares,
and you want to get away
from the madness,
you just call My name
and I'll be there.

Mac Powell, Third Day, *Call My Name*

The genesis of the journey which led him to the clearing experience occurred slightly more than a year earlier. On a Tuesday in May, with bluebird skies and bright sun overhead, Dean Moone went to see Dr. Max Johnson about a small lump on his neck that he had noticed sometime around Christmas of the previous year. It seemed to be a swollen gland, and he really hadn't put much thought into it, except that Krista demonstrated uncanny "wife radar," and had kept bugging him about getting it checked. It didn't hurt or anything; it just wasn't going away.

After a five-minute physical exam and initial blood work, Dr. Johnson informed Dean that several of his lymph nodes were swollen, and additional testing needed to be done. The technicians poked, prodded, scanned, stuck, and then painstakingly recorded every detail of the whole process. Dean felt like a lab rat, and the underlying uneasiness about the nature of the tests gnawed at his gut. It was decided that the following week, Dean would venture back to see Dr. Johnson, and discuss the results of the blood work, CAT scans, and chest x-rays.

Now, Dean sat flipping through a year-old copy of *Field and Stream*, trying to lose himself in an article about fishing for smallmouth bass in creeks, when the doctor tapped twice on the metal door and entered the room. He perched himself opposite Dean on a swivel stool and scooted it within three feet or so of the exam table where Dean sat. There was no small talk, no niceties. Dean waited silently, utterly unprepared for the turn the conversation then took. Dr. Johnson floored Dean in a way no one ever had in his life. He had come into the room with a poker face, but his eyes now revealed concern.

"There's no good way to say this, Dean," the doctor began. "I'm reasonably sure you have a form of cancer of the lymph system." He paused, looking at Dean's test results again, flipping through pages on the chart, more for a moment's distraction than to further confirm what he already knew.

This remained the part of medicine Max Johnson hoped he never grew numb to—it was still good, in his mind, that this type of news was difficult for him to deliver. Clearing his throat, the doctor continued, "Though we can't know for sure without additional blood work and a biopsy, my suspicion is that it could be Hodgkin's disease, a very curable form of cancer."

Even as Max Johnson explained everything to him, Dean found

a calm settled over him about this news. He was overwhelmed, to be sure, but somehow calm at the same time. He found himself anxious to get on with the rest of the blood work and the biopsy.

Dean decided at that moment not to tell Krista much, other than that he had a swollen gland and that Dr. Johnson wanted to take a closer look to see what was going on. *No need to worry her,* he thought, *until we know what exactly we're fighting.*

Dean drove home in silence after scheduling the biopsy appointment with Dr. Johnson's nurse. He had to come back the next morning, and also had a lot to get his head around on the way home. His mind raced over all the details she outlined for him, as the wheels rolled over the interstate.

The drive from downtown Atlanta back out to Marietta was just long enough for him to gather his thoughts about how to deal with finally explaining everything to Krista. He admitted to himself that he felt guilty for not being completely open and honest from the onset. Their marriage had always been based on trust, and he knew that withholding this type of information was unlike him. Dean just didn't want to sound the big "C" alarm until it was confirmed one hundred percent. Nothing was confirmed until the biopsy, and he didn't have all the facts yet. His years in the real estate business had made him a man who could expertly assess a situation, facing a challenge head-on. He wanted all the facts to build out his battle plan. Dean had built his successful commercial real estate group from scratch. His knack for understanding people, their needs and personalities, proved to be a great asset as he developed his clientele. It didn't hurt that he was so personable himself, but he also had a keen insight on how the competition operated, and thrived on closing a big, hard-fought deal. He wasn't known for being one to back down from a challenge, and he determined this would not be the time to start, either. There was a reason this particular course of events began to unfold at this time. He knew this, believed this. What he didn't know yet was what the reason was, and what the journey would entail.

His thoughts turning back to the road, he gripped the steering wheel more tightly and prayed out loud in the traffic. "Dear Lord," he began, "I have no idea why You've set my feet upon this path. I need to see Your hand in this, and feel Your presence in this. Don't let me forget You are the One who will see me through this. *Please*," his voice cracked, "bless me with strength for the battle ahead, and peace."

Peace. It was something Dean suspected he would pray for many times over in the coming days, weeks, and months. There was an impending sense that something significant loomed on the horizon. Something that he never could have imagined. Dean was pensive, anxious.

His mind drifted to the Psalms. Their words had comforted him through so many difficulties over the years. This reassurance had sprung from a conversation with a young minister years earlier, just after Dean's father died. Dean spent his first two years at college at the University of South Carolina, pursuing a business degree.

When his father was diagnosed with advanced colon cancer in the fall of his sophomore year, Dean returned home to help his mother care for him. He was grateful for the time with his dad, but was full of the same questions most kids his age struggled with from time to time. Watching Big Bob die of cancer had infuriated Dean, not only because he didn't want to lose his dad, but also because it had made him feel so powerless. In the end, there was nothing he or his mother could do but hold those gentle, giant hands and tell them they loved him. For several months after that, Dean had struggled to make sense of it all. Some days he failed miserably. The day he sat down with that young minister had been one of the more trying days, and years later, Dean realized perhaps that was one reason their conversation had made such an impact.

Mike Owens had explained that, as a student of scripture and leader of a congregation, he'd slowly gained an understanding and insight into the heart of the Psalms and why they were written. From his perspective, it basically took the pressure off any expectation of human perfection. The pastor's confidence of this rested in the fact that he understood that David, the shepherd-turned-king who penned the Psalms, was a mess. He was a true screw-up really, full of pride and many other human faults. Pastor Mike explained to Dean that it was actually in David's *weakness* that he ultimately found his strength.

"So," he had confessed to Dean while enjoying a glass of tea one afternoon, "the testament of David the Psalmist is that God is truly our Deliverer. If we cry out from the depths of sheer agony in our circumstances, when we have absolutely nothing left, God is still there, and defends us and cares for us." He added, "He truly will meet you wherever you are."

Dean had rocked in his chair on his parents' front porch and peered over the railing. "Well, I'll admit I identify with the being a mess and having faults part. I guess that *is* comforting in some weird way. But, what do you mean about meeting us 'where we are'?"

"Well," Pastor Mike said, "it means a lot of people think they have to have everything wrapped up in some neat little package to 'present' to God; that He only wants to see us at our best."

This perplexed Dean. "Isn't that what we're trying to do, though?" he asked.

Mike nodded. "Yes," he said. "But we're on the way, Dean, to being better. God's with us at our worst, too."

"Then why is that when we feel so *alone*?" Dean asked.

The pastor shrugged his shoulders. "My experience is that in those times most of us are afraid to turn to God. We don't want to admit we're broken, even to the only One who can begin putting us back together."

Dean fell silent, thinking on the young minister's last comments.

Pastor Mike had pushed a little further. "So, going back to the Psalms, only by turning over all of his *deepest* fears and most painful wounds could David's soul begin to be healed. Dean," he paused, "that means you need to understand that nothing you say or do is gonna shock God. Or chase Him away. Not ever. He's in it with you for the good, the bad, *and* the ugly."

He had to roll it around for a few days, but in Dean's college-aged mind, this had ultimately brought a level of comfort he could cling to, after the doubts began to subside.

Back in the present, the words of Psalm 27 drummed through his head to the rhythm of the wheels turning on the Georgia asphalt.

...though the war should rise up against me,

yet will I put my trust in him.

Chapter 3

Each friend represents a world in us,
a world possibly not born until they arrive,
and it is only by this meeting
that a new world is born.

Anais Nin

It was going to be a long night.

Dean tried to act as normal as possible during dinner and the rest of the evening. He seemed a little preoccupied, but thankfully Krista had been busy grading a stack of tests and homework most of the night. This distraction and her need to prepare lesson plans for the following week provided the respite from conversation Dean desperately needed. He had casually mentioned some follow up at the doctor, but made sure to speak in general terms, with few details, and went to bed feeling that although he'd not been completely honest with Krista about the extent of the tests, he had at least let her know he was going back. It bought him some more time. They were both exhausted by the time the nightly news was over, and they turned in without much fanfare.

The next morning, Dean arrived at the outpatient side of the clinic promptly at seven a.m. Because of the location and size of the node, the biopsy could be done under local anesthetic, so he had not needed to bring anyone with him. The prepping took twice as long as the procedure itself, and Dean was on his way to his office before nine. Dr. Johnson had informed him that they would have the tests back in a few days, and his nurse would call to schedule an appointment to review the results.

He dialed Jimmy Carlton's number on the way to the office. Since eighth grade, Jimmy had been Dean's buddy. Best friend. They'd grown up together, meeting for the first time on the football field, and adding more activities and adventures over the years. Every chance they'd had, chances were they were out fishing, climbing trees, and planning new schemes. This current "adventure" did not bring out the childlike anticipation in Dean, and he needed a break, a distraction.

Jimmy's voice beamed through the line, "Well, hey there, stranger!"

"Hey, Jimmy, what's new?" Dean managed to get out with a nonchalant air.

"Oh, you know, same stuff, different day," came the reply. "What's shakin' with you?"

"I need to go fishing," Dean blurted. "Thinking about heading up to the lake this afternoon, taking the tent, and hitting the bass hard this evening and again in the morning. You game?" Dean knew the response before he asked the question.

"Are you kidding?" Jimmy laughed. "I know you are *not* even wastin' breath askin' me *that* question. What time you planning on heading out?"

"I'm thinking around four o'clock," said Dean. "Meet me at my house?"

"You got it, man. See you then." There was a short pause. "Hey, Dean," said Jimmy. "Something up?"

"Nah," Dean lied. "Just need to feel something tugging on the end of a line. See you at four."

Jimmy's truck pulled up in front of Dean's house at 3:50. Restraining himself from arriving at three o'clock had posed a huge challenge, and Dean smiled when his friend climbed out and met him in the driveway. They shook hands and Jimmy fell right in step with Dean, filling coolers, slinging tackle boxes in Dean's truck, and pulling last minute supplies together. Once everything was loaded to their satisfaction, they grabbed a couple of sodas from the cooler and hopped in the cab of the truck.

Gus, Dean's German shepherd, waited impatiently on the small backseat of the extended cab, tail wagging and legs pacing, but he settled in quickly as the wheels rolled over the highway. For several years, Dean had taken Gus with him on most of his fishing trips, to the point an angling adventure seemed incomplete without the dog's presence.

The beat-up, green Toyota truck made it out of town quickly and soon bumped along the country roads on the way to the pair's favorite bass lake. The warm May nights had raised the water temperature, and Dean longed to sling some topwater lures to see how feisty the bass were feeling. On the occasional bump or pothole in the road, Gus would utter a faint growl or grunt, then shove his nose back down under his forepaw with a sigh.

Upon arrival, and following the setup of camp, the two friends quickly grabbed their tackle and headed toward the lakeshore, with

Gus following close behind. The afternoon breeze warmed them, and the lingering sunshine made it possible for them to fish well into evening. Topwater baits sailed through the air and splashed on the surface of the water. For Dean and Jimmy, nothing matched the thrill of teasing a bass to the surface. Cast after cast, large baits with crazy names like Hula Popper and Lucky 13 splashed onto the water's surface and chugged back toward the bank, leaving a wake behind them. The anglers worked the banks and fallen logs hard, enticing bass from their hiding places. The quiet gurgle of the baits along the surface was interrupted on occasion by a sound akin to a toilet flushing, with a flurry of activity, as a fish struck the lure. They laughed and chided one another, landing a few nice-size lunkers.

Dean was grateful for the time with Jimmy and the distraction offered by the afternoon's activities. Just before dark, they changed to smaller rods and baits, deciding to hit the bream for a while. Coming on the eve of a full moon, the bream fishing proved fast and furious, and they decided to keep a few of the slab bluegills for dinner that night.

"Man," said Jimmy, "I can't wait to throw these in that skillet over there."

Dean had already started cleaning the fish, tossing them in the cooler when he had finished, while Jimmy started the fire. He nodded. "Don't I know it! You started slicing those onions and potatoes yet? Or do I have to do *everything*?" Gus, who'd already tried to eat the remains from the earlier fish cleaning, danced in excited anticipation of the cooking.

Over dinner, Dean related the day's events at the doctor's office with his friend. Jimmy asked a few questions here and there, between shoveled bites of hush puppies and fish, but mostly listened.

"So Krista doesn't know any of this right now?" he asked Dean, throwing back a large swig of Coke and wiping his mouth with the back of this hand.

Dean shook his head. "Nope, and you know I don't usually keep things from her. Believe me, Jim, I don't take any of this lightly. I just would rather know what we're really up against before I scare her to death."

Jimmy understood. He agreed with Dean, reaching for the last hush puppy, and adding, "I get it, and I think she will too. Really."

"I'll know more early next week," Dean concluded. "Then I have a feeling we *all* may know more than we want to." He looked Jimmy in the eye. "Now," he said, "can we please get some more fish in the skillet? I'm still hungry!"

Gus wagged his tail and barked his enthusiastic accord.

Chapter 4

Over every mountain
there is a path,
although it may not be seen
from the valley.

James D. Rogers

While fishing with Jimmy, Dean had come to grips with the fact that he had cancer. He had even reached an inexplicable peace about it, and began formulating a battle plan that included all the prayer warriors he could recruit, all the faith he could summon. But the results of the biopsy confirmed Dean's worst fears and delivered more horrible news than he could have imagined.

The details bombarded him at his next appointment. It turned out to be non-Hodgkin's lymphoma, a malignant cancer of the lymph system, and Dr. Johnson explained that there were some things about the biopsy that would have to be further investigated by an oncologist. The explanation was complicated, but the main thrust was that, unfortunately, Dean's particular version on the disease didn't involve just a few lymph nodes, but the *entire* lymph system from head to thigh.

Dean peeked at his chart while Dr. Johnson stepped out to take a call. *Nodular poorly differentiated lymphocytic lymphoma, with indications of T cell and B cell corruption and bone marrow invasion, Stage IV.* He hardly needed a medical degree to understand the gravity of the situation. Eighty-four percent of white blood cells *cancerous.* All lymph nodes *cancerous.* Bone marrow *cancerous.* Dean felt lightheaded, and a wave of nausea swept over him.

Dr. Johnson had his nurse immediately schedule an appointment with an oncologist. Dean committed the name of Dr. Gray Richards to memory, and left with a card reminding him of the upcoming meeting. As he got into his car, Dean knew he would now have to break the news to Krista. He prayed, wrestling with the best way to tell her about what they were about to face.

"I have no idea what to say," he whispered. "Please, Lord, help me break this to her in a way that does her—and You—justice."

He arrived at home, and much to Dean's surprise, Krista's car sat in the driveway. Choosing not to linger, he marched resolutely up the sidewalk.

"Hey, there," Krista greeted when he swung open the kitchen door.

"Hey, yourself," came the reply.

Krista's eyes squinted and the right corner of her mouth pulled back the way it always did when she was considering something intently. "Something's up—what is it?"

Dean closed his eyes and bit at his mustache with his lower teeth, willing himself to say the words. He set his keys on the counter and turned to face her. "Honey," he began, "I've just gotten all the final test results back from Dr. Johnson." He tried to clear his throat, but his voice faltered, and Krista began to cry. She knew the next part of the conversation before her husband said another word.

"It's bad, isn't it?" she asked.

"Krista, I..."

"*Cancer*?" she whispered.

He nodded.

She shook her head back and forth, vehemently trying to dislodge the words from her mind. "No!" she cried. "We are *not* having this conversation...oh, please...tell me we're not really having this conversation." She melted into his arms as the reality permeated her being.

Dean cried, too. And they stood there, in the kitchen, holding each other and crying for several minutes. He studied the blue and white flowers on the curtains hanging over the kitchen sink. He stroked Krista's hair, and she buried her face in his chest. When they both regained a small semblance of composure, they sat down at the kitchen table. Dean reached for her hand, though neither said a word. They just stared at each other, praying their own silent prayers.

Krista broke the silence first. "So," she said, wiping under her lower lashes with the knuckles of her index fingers, "what's next?"

"A follow-up appointment with an oncologist," he answered. "Gray Richards. I'm honestly not sure what all the next steps are yet. I mean, I know just having the basic diagnosis is serious, but we're a little light on details at this point. I think we just have to take one step at a time."

Krista's eyes welled again as a new thought emerged. She

sucked in a breath. "Oh, God," she gasped, her hands flying to her chest. "What about Maggie?"

Dean nodded as he considered their daughter. "I thought about that on the way home, too," he admitted quietly. "School's out in a few weeks. Why don't we go see Dr. Richards together first and then tell her when summer vacation starts?"

"Yeah," Krista sighed, "I think that's probably a good idea. She sat back in her chair and added, "Besides, how do you decide when it's a good time to tell a second grader her dad has cancer anyway?"

As expected, Dr. Richards ran more tests at the next appointment, and confirmed the diagnosis of non-Hodgkin's lymphoma. Though Dean's disease was not in an overly aggressive mode at that point in time, the doctor informed him it had indeed advanced well into stage IV.

And from that point, Dean's medical education commenced, advancing at a rapid rate. He learned doctors weren't really sure what caused non-Hodgkin's lymphoma, but they knew it occurred when the body produced too many abnormal lymphocytes—a type of white blood cell. Normally, lymphocytes go through a predictable life cycle. Old lymphocytes die, and the body creates new ones to replace them. In Dean's case, his lymphocytes didn't die, but rather, continued to grow and divide. This oversupply of lymphocytes crowded into his lymph nodes, causing them to swell. Dean then understood why he had a knot that wouldn't go away.

They learned that non-Hodgkin's lymphoma generally involves the presence of cancerous lymphocytes in the lymph nodes, but the disease can also spread to other parts of the lymphatic system. These, Dr.

Richards explained, included the lymphatic vessels, tonsils, adenoids, spleen, thymus and bone marrow.

"Dean," said the doctor, "yours has invaded your bone marrow." Dean also remembered from what his father went through with colon cancer that doctors also assign a stage (I through IV) to the disease, based on the number of tumors and how widely the tumors had spread. The fact that his had been diagnosed at Stage IV was *not* what Dean wanted to hear.

"At this time," the doctor explained, "there is no confirmed cure for this type of cancer in the late stages like yours."

Dean was taken aback. "So, what does that mean?"

"Frankly, the fact that it is *not* very aggressive right now makes it more difficult to recommend a specific course of treatment." The doctor clenched his jaw and looked at Dean and Krista. "Ultimately," he concluded, "it's your decision. It's my job to be sure you to have all the facts. You need to know one thing, though," he said. "As it stands right now, without treatment your chances for survival at this stage in the progression of the disease are virtually non-existent."

Krista gasped. Dean stared at the doctor, and grabbed his wife's hand. "Non-existent, huh? Wow."

"What about *with* treatment?" Krista inquired. "What does that do to his chances?"

Gray Richards clasped his hands in front of him across the table from the couple. "To tell you the truth," he said, "I honestly don't know. None of the standard treatments I'd normally suggest could even be considered at this point; the protocols would require it to have begun much earlier in the advancement of the lymphoma. I do know of a couple of experimental trials at other hospitals. It's a long shot, but I can make some inquiries and get you some information to consider."

Dean and Krista looked from each other back to the doctor and both nodded. Dean spoke first. "Yes, please," he said. "We need to know every single option we have. Those odds aren't something I'm willing to accept right now." His voice faltered. "I just want to be clear. You're basically saying I'm *terminal*, aren't you?"

A small cry involuntarily escaped from the back of Krista's throat at the mention of the word, and she clapped her hand over her mouth, willing it silent.

The doctor rolled his pen back and forth between his thumb and forefinger, considering his answer. "If you choose not to pursue any of the experimental treatments, I'd say you can possibly expect to live another six to eight months, but one never knows for certain."

The Patient Advocate at the doctor's office armed the couple with several pamphlets, phone numbers and even a video as they finally left the appointment. The doctor realized he'd given them an overwhelming amount of information to digest in a short time, and he urged them to take the time they needed to process it all.

"You need to act quickly," Dr. Richards advised. "But a few days isn't going to drastically alter anything. This is a big decision."

After reviewing all the options over the next few days, Dean and Krista decided that, mainly because of Dean's young age of only thirty-seven, they would opt for the experimental program. A radical, aggressive chemotherapy treatment program sponsored by one particular hospital in the Midwest.

"After all, what do I have to lose?" Dean asked after they had made the decision. "I have *two* great reasons to beat this cancer," he said, pulling his wife close to him. "One is thirty-eight, and the other will be eight in July."

Krista smiled through her tears.

"I'm not sure exactly how He did it, Honey," Dean said, "but I want to be sure you know that God has somehow prepared me so well for this. I get the verse now about 'the peace that passes understanding.'"

"So, you're saying you're *ready* for this?" she asked him. "That you accept this?"

"No," he replied. "What I'm saying is I sure don't even understand what all of this is at this point, but I'm peaceful about it."

"Oh, great," she said, rolling her eyes, "now that makes perfect sense!"

That night, after Krista went to bed, Dean drafted a letter to their Sunday School class. Theirs was a tight-knit group, one that had survived many struggles together through the years. He wanted to let them know he believed in the strength of their prayers, the strength of their friendship, and also that he believed in his ability to beat his diagnosis, regardless of how grim it seemed in the present. When he finished editing and saving it on his computer, the final printout read:

To my Sunday School class,

As most of you know by now, I have cancer. It is called non-Hodgkin's lymphoma, which is a malignant cancer of the lymph system. Unfortunately, we've learned the entire lymph system is involved and not just a few nodes. We also know at this point that it is well advanced into stage IV, and it is a cancer with no known cure. The unknown at this point is the treatment, I will undergo. The answers to these questions will be determined this week, since all the reports and testing are now complete.

It seems that I have fought many battles in my life, some before I met Krista, and some since then. This time the battle is different—I'm literally battling for my life. And a little bit to my surprise, this has been one of the easiest for me to prepare for. I did struggle with the initial surprise of the news from the doctor and with trying to figure out how to tell Krista, but I have come to a great peace that I do not understand. What I do understand is that God can handle anything, even when I think I can't

The side effects are pretty much guaranteed: 1) Nausea and vomiting, 2) loss of my hair, and 3) infections that may hospitalize me two or three times over the six- to eight-month therapy. I've gotta tell you, I'm looking as forward to the chemotherapy as you would look forward to swimming naked in a pool full of poison-ivy juice. So, the way I see it, we can only have 3 outcomes: 1) to be healed by God instantly, 2) to be healed by God through the doctors and chemotherapy, and 3) to have ultimate healing through death. I've decided I can live with any of those options.

After the next Sunday's class, the group was sharing their usual coffee hour when one particular class member walked up to Dean. "You know," she said, patting him on the back, "I had an uncle *and* a cousin who had lymphoma."

"Really?" said Dean.

"Yeah, not at the same time, of course," she laughed, "but yes, both of them had what you have," she offered.

"Well," replied Dean, raising his eyebrows, "so, how are they doing now?"

"Oh," she said nonchalantly, waving her hand in the air, "they both died."

Dean closed his eyes tightly, reopened them and just smiled. "Thanks a lot," he said, reaching for the coffee pot. "Well, we'll see you next week." She waved over her shoulder as she walked back across the room and disappeared by the muffins.

Over the coming weeks and months, Dean found that friends and others he encountered typically fell into one of three categories. The first group couldn't stand any amount of silence. They usually said the first thing to come to their minds, regardless of whether it was truly comforting or not. Dean knew they didn't speak from a lack of compassion, but because their hearts compelled them to fill the silence. Others tried too hard to find just the right words to share with Dean. "We're praying for you," they would say. Or, "Our thoughts are with you and your family." Now, all of these were welcomed and appreciated, to be sure, and Dean knew the intentions were good. The last group fell nearest to Dean's heart, for they were the ones who readily admitted they simply had no idea what to say. He also did his best to let them know it wasn't necessary to say *anything*. The epitome of this played out the next day, when a friend stopped by the house after hearing the news.

When Dean opened the door Jack King did not move.

"Can I give you a hug?" Jack asked.

Dean just smiled and opened his arms. They embraced briefly, and Dean invited him into his home. The exchanged some small talk that didn't last long.

"Dean, I don't need to stay," Jack said. "I just wanted you to know I was thinking about you."

Dean nodded.

"Is it okay if I cry?" asked Jack.

Again, a nod. Dean sat with his friend in silence, two men nearing forty, both former athletes who were tall and strong, and both openly letting tears stream down their faces.

"I have no words, but I still had to come," he finally said.

"You know," Dean replied, "I'm finding that it's really okay to *not* know what to say. I just really appreciate you taking the time to come."

This, he found, rang true. Wrong words, too many words, or no words at all, just to know others cared meant something, even if they had no idea how to express it.

Chapter 5

Keep me as the apple of your eye.

Psalm 17:8

Margaret Elizabeth Moone sat cross-legged in the middle of her bedroom floor. A multitude of Barbie dolls surrounded her while she carried on simultaneous conversations with all of them. As an only child, she loved making up new games and adventures, and days such as these marked some of her favorite times. She could entertain herself for hours. For all of her eight years, Maggie was quite a creative presenter, and her fun often involved plays, songs, Barbie dramas, and lots of giggles. She was the apple of Dean's eye, and their kinship was a powerful bond.

Dean stood in the hallway, just out of his daughter's line of sight; he could watch her while she remained oblivious to his presence, engrossed in her playtime. This would be a day neither of them would forget, and his mind kept wandering to other days with Maggie that were also burned into his memory.

A couple of months earlier, for instance, Dean had initiated Maggie into the more-advanced angling club with a trip to his favorite trout creek in northern Georgia. In the foothills of the Appalachian mountains, near Dahlonega, the Moone family cabin welcomed father and daughter to true adventure. Dahlonega is nestled in the foot hills of the Blue Ridge Mountains, and one-third of the county is in the Chattahoochee National Forest, making the area a great place for trout fishing. Big Bob had built the cabin himself when Dean was about Maggie's age, and the cabin's convenient, centralized location meant that most local trout streams were easily accessible. Various creeks contained combinations of stocked rainbow and wild rainbow and brown trout, although the trophy-trout streams continued to suffer from the presence of otters, which put a serious dent in the population.

Dean's favorite, Noontootla Creek, was formed by the confluence of Stover Creek, Chester Creek and Long Creek and flowed through a part of the Blue Ridge Wildlife Management Area known as the Three Forks Area. What made Noontootla Creek and its tributaries favorites of Dean's was that they weren't stocked with hatchery fish and were actively managed by local conservation groups to imitate natural streams, with an unharvested trout population. The waters were also open throughout the year. Because the trout in Noontootla weren't "dough bellies," the common slang for hatchery trout, the fishing was more challenging, and he appreciated the fish he caught around Three Forks more because of it. If he planned to supplement Maggie's angling experience, this would be a great place to start. She'd already caught bream and small bass in some of the area's stocked lakes on previous trips, so she felt special to get to go up to the creeks in pursuit of her first trout.

They'd spent the night before at the cabin, so they could rise just before the sun and make it to their favorite café for breakfast. Dean enjoyed a second cup of coffee while Maggie made an astute observation, noting their goal would have been to be on the water before dawn if they were chasing bass rather than trout.

"Do trout sleep later, Daddy?" she asked.

"I'm not sure fish actually *sleep*, Buga Bear," he laughed, "but trout do eat a little differently than bass." He spooned a mouthful of grits into his mouth for emphasis. "You finish your pancakes, and we'll go get 'em, okay?"

"Okay, Daddy," she grinned, and shoved an oversized bite of syrup-laden pancakes in her mouth. Maggie loved days like this, getting to eat pancakes with too much syrup and laughing with her dad. She watched him get up to pay the bill and walk back to the table. She slurped the last drops of orange juice from the bottom of her glass and wiped her mouth with the paper napkin.

"Ready, Buga Bear?" Dean asked.

"Ready!"

They headed north out of Dahlonega on Highway 19, winding for another eight or ten miles to the entrance of the Ranger Training Camp, from where they followed the Forest Service roads, continuing to the top of the ridge at Winding Stair Gap. These roads had made Dean's knuckles white when he was a kid, banging along in the truck with his dad. He would peer out the passenger window as they rounded the sharp curves, certain at any moment that the truck would just lurch right off the edge of the road and plummet into the creek below. About the time he was eight or nine, he'd seen an old beat up car lodged in a tree halfway down the face of the canyon, and even in adulthood, the image was frighteningly vivid for Dean. The memory caused the hair to stand up on the back of Dean's neck, and he gripped the wheel a bit tighter for good measure. A couple of miles down the other side of the ridge, they made it to the Three Forks Area at the bottom of the mountain.

Most of his early fishing time with Big Bob and Ted in these waters occurred with a spinning rod in his hand. Later, in his early teens, they'd all tried their hands at fly fishing during certain times of the year, but Dean knew many different ways existed to catch a trout, and today's goal was for Maggie to do just that. Dean had brought along an ultralight spinning rod for Maggie in addition to his 4-weight fly rod. He knew all too well that, at her age, it was important for her to develop a love of the sport, including the thrill of actually hooking a fish. Whether she enticed it with a fly rod or spinning rod was irrelevant. They hiked down the foot trail from the parking area, and Dean found a nice open area on the bank near a pool overhung by a tree. The location of the tree would not hamper a cast, only aid them in their quest because it provided shadows and cover for the lurking trout.

He'd tied on a long, light leader the night before, and now added some 4X tippet. He explained everything to Maggie as he went, showing her different sizes of clear line, and telling her how tippet was an extra piece of line tied on to make the lure look more like it was not attached to anything in the water.

"These trout are a little spooky," he told her. "If we can use some light tippet we'll have a better chance of fooling the fish."

Maggie nodded enthusiastically, and maintained her intent

gaze on her father's hands. She watched as he then tied a small Yellow Stonefly, a size 16, to the tippet. As he again explained his steps to Maggie, she remained engaged in the conversation, asking several questions for clarification as they continued.

"What do the numbers mean, Daddy? Like a 'size 16,' what is that?"

Dean looked over the rims of his sunglasses at a curious freckled face. "Well, Bugs, the higher the number, the smaller the fly," he explained, pinching his fingers closely together and holding them up to show a small size.

"But that's backwards."

Dean nodded. "Yes, it is," he agreed, "but here, let me show you something." He opened his fly box and sat down on a log next to Maggie. Pointing to various flies, he explained the differences in terrestrials, such as beetles, and dry flies, like the Light Cahill he hoped to use later in the day. The terrestrials lived on the land, but often landed in the water to be eaten by a fish, like a grasshopper jumping a little too far or getting carried by the wind. Some flies looked big and bushy, with hairs that stood straight up like wings on their backs, while others looked to Maggie like someone had just wound string around a bare hook. It was a pretty basic conversation, with Dean being careful not to get too technical and douse his daughter's spark of interest.

"So," he said slapping his thigh, "shall we give it a shot?"

Maggie nodded enthusiastically. "Can I just watch for a few minutes and see how you do it?" she asked. "I'm thinking this might be a lot different than that pond we fished in before."

Dean smiled and tousled her strawberry blonde hair. "Bugs, I think that's a great suggestion."

He made his way along the bank, a few feet from Maggie so he could roll cast to the run leading into the pool. The plan was not to disturb the pool, but to see if at least they were biting. He wanted to leave the pool undisturbed for his partner. A dozen or so upstream casts, with the stonefly imitation bouncing along in the current, finally produced a decent fish, about 14 inches long. Dean and Maggie marveled at the colors and markings before gently releasing it back into the clear water.

"That was COOL!" giggled Maggie.

"I totally agree," her dad replied. "Now, it's your turn."

Her eyes widened. "I don't know if I can do that thing you did. Whatdya call it? A rolled cat?"

Dean laughed. "A roll cast," he said. "You use it when you can't cast backwards because of trees or other things in the way behind you, and you're right, it can get a little tricky. That's why we also brought this." He reached down by their gear and handed Maggie the ultralight rod. After Maggie had gone to bed the night before, Dean had sat at his fly-tying table and modified a couple of spinners for her. Tied on the line was a small Rooster Tail lure. Dean had taken off the treble hook on the back and replaced it with a single hook, pinching down the barb since he knew they were in trophy water with barbless regulations.

"All for you, Bugs," he said. "You remember how to cast it, right? So just walk to the edge of the creek and try to land your cast just on this side of that little pool there." He pointed to the head of the pool with his fly rod while his other hand rested across her shoulders.

"And I'll catch a fish?"

"Hopefully," he said, "but it might take a few tries, okay?"

She nodded, already lost in concentration.

"Just let it sink and float all the way through the pool before you start to reel it back in."

Maggie listened to her dad, and after flubbing the first cast, which landed the lure—*splat*—about two feet in front of her, she got the hang of it again quickly. On the sixth cast, the Rooster Tail pierced the water a foot above the head of the pool, and sank slowly with the current, and drifted through the pool, and stopped. She thought she'd snagged a branch or something, and started to reel back in when Dean let out a whoop.

"You've got one, Bugs!"

The line wiggled back and forth, the trout shaking its head trying to free the hook.

"Don't let the line go slack; just keep reeling and you'll be fine."

She dug the butt end of the rod into her tummy, holding the rod in her left hand and reeling steadily with her right. The trout came in a bit, and then turned and took out line again on a run. She laughed and squealed while Dean watched carefully, but allowed his daughter to relish the experience all on her own. "You're doing great," he'd called. "Easy now, he's still on there. You've got it."

Her eight-year-old frame held a determined posture. She listened to her father, and just kept reeling the trout toward her. Reeling. Reeling. Run. Reeling. Reeling. Run. Soon, the fish began to tire, slowing its run, making it easier for Maggie to reel.

"Just keep reeling, Bugs, while I get the net," Dean instructed over his shoulder.

"Okay," she said. "*Got 'im*!"

When Dean turned back around with the net, he started laughing so hard tears streamed down his cheeks. "Well now," he said through breaths, "I'll say you got him!"

Standing on the bank of the creek, grinning from ear to ear, Maggie's rod tip was still in the water, but with her inaugural rainbow trout reeled all the way up to the tip-top guide! She had reeled until she couldn't reel any farther without forcing the trout's nose through the guides. She'd been careful not to take the rod tip out of the water for fear the fish wouldn't be able to breathe.

Dean quickly flipped the bail on the reel to let out a little line so they could release the trout without injury. He gently unhooked the fish, and Maggie bent down to see it.

"Wet your hands first and you can hold him before we release him," he told her.

Maggie dunked her hands and took the fish from her father. It was slippery, but she was able to hold on long enough for Dean to take a photo. The photo still sat in a frame on his desk.

"Daddy?"

"Helloooo…Dad!" Maggie stood in front of him, waving her hand back and forth in front of Dean's face. She narrowed her eyes. "Were you spying on me?"

"What?" He roused himself from his memories. "No, Buga Bear," he answered, "not spying, just watching, and enjoying your playtime."

She looked up at him skeptically, brushing a lock of hair from in front of her big hazel eyes, and asked, "You wanna play, too?"

Dean laughed. "No, Bugs, but thanks. Just not today."

"Oh, okay," she said, and turned to rejoin her Barbies.

"But Maggie," Dean reached to gently take her arm and turn her around to him again, "I did want to talk to you about something."

"What?"

"Well, do you think we could sit down a minute?"

"Okay," she said. "Wanna sit on the bed or the floor?"

"Whatever you want is fine with me," he said.

She flopped back down. "Floor."

And it was there, seated cross-legged amidst Barbie dolls and clothes and cars, Dean told his eight-year-old only child that he had cancer.

Chapter 6

"For I know the plans I have for you,"
declares the LORD,
"plans to prosper you and not to harm you,
plans to give you hope and a future."

Jeremiah 29:11

Dean left Maggie to her dolls and joined Krista in the den. She sat waiting for Dean in the overstuffed chair he'd given her two Christmases prior, while tears gently spilled over her lashes onto her cheeks. When Dean entered the room, she wiped her cheeks with the backs of her hands and sat up straighter in the chair.

"So," she said softly, "how'd she take it?"

Dean just shook his head as he sat in the chair next to hers. "She's a pretty amazing kid, you know that?"

"I do know."

Dean and Krista had agreed that once Dean's treatment protocol had been established, they mustn't try to keep his illness a secret from Maggie. She was an intelligent and intuitive child, and they felt that seeing the changes in him as he endured the treatment and transplant could potentially frighten her more than knowing her father was sick.

He related to Krista the general course of the conversation with Maggie, how he'd told her that the knot in his neck was more than just a knot, that he had cancer, and that it was a type that made your blood sick. He also told her that he would be getting a lot of different kinds of medicines for a few months to see if his blood could get better on its own, and that if it couldn't, then the doctors would have to try to give him some new parts to make new, healthy blood.

Maggie had listened intently, tears welling in her big hazel eyes, trying to understand Dean's over-simplified explanation of non-Hodgkin's lymphoma and how a bone marrow transplant might work. As she struggled to grasp it all, Dean asked her if she had any questions she wanted to ask him.

"Just one," she said very matter-of-factly.

"Okay, shoot."

"Is it the kind of cancer people die from?" She knew that her grandfather, whom she never met, had died of cancer, and some of her other friends' relatives as well. At that point Maggie was far less concerned with which type Dean had or what the treatments were than if it was a kind that would take her father away from her.

Dean just stared blankly at her. He felt like he'd been hit in the stomach with a sledgehammer. What could he say? How could he say it? He didn't know why some people died and others did not. "Some people do, Bugs," he said, "but Mom and I have thought about that and prayed about that a lot lately, and I honestly don't think I will."

"Daddy?"

"Yes, honey?"

"There's something I don't understand. Why do they give you

the medicine first, before they give you a new way to make the good blood?" To Maggie, this seemed to be the reverse of what she expected, and if her dad was going to have to endure horrible medicines that made him feel even worse, she wanted to know why.

Dean cleared his throat. "That's a really good question, so let me see if I can give you an honest answer," he said. "It's sorta hard to explain, Bugs, but the way the doctors explained it to me is like this... they have to give me the strong medicine first to kill all the cancer that's already made my blood sick. If they didn't, and they just did the transplant to help make new healthy blood, that new blood would just get sick too." He paused to let the first part of the explanation sink in.

Maggie twirled a strand of amber hair around her finger, the way she usually did when she fell deep in thought, or was sleepy. "Okay," she agreed, "but after they give you the medicine, if it works really good, will you still have to have the other thing? What is it called, a *trans-plant*?" she enunciated each syllable to ensure she remembered it correctly.

"Yes," he answered. "See, once they get rid of all the bad cells, it will get rid of some of the good ones too. I'll need the transplant so I can make all the good kind I need once the bad ones are all gone." He hoisted her onto his lap and squeezed her shoulders. "Does that make sense?"

"I guess," she admitted distractedly. "It just sounds to me like you're gonna have to take icky medicine that doesn't really make you better, just so you can have an operation. At least when I don't want to take the icky medicine, Mom gets me to do it by telling me it will make me *all* better."

Dean laughed. She was right. The road ahead seemed long and confusing to him, too, but he trusted the doctors to give him the best treatment based on the gravity of his prognosis. The one thing he knew for sure was doing *nothing* wasn't an option. He had to fight with everything he had. "I'm still a little confused too, Honey," he admitted. "We may have to learn some of it together. And I know there'll be times we're all scared. But we have good doctors, good insurance, and one really super thing on our side."

"Oh, I know!" she said excitedly. "*God's* on our side, right, Dad?"

"Yep!"

Then she completely changed the course of the conversation. "Daddy," she asked, out of the blue, "do you think God knew what was going to happen and that's why He let all those things with your business go bad?"

Dean pondered the question. His daughter displayed acuity beyond her years. Over the course of the previous nine to twelve months, an unforeseen series of events had transpired, forcing Dean to make the decision to close his business. His business didn't "go bad,"as Maggie phrased it, but that was the general gist, and she knew things were different. The funny thing was the final outcome really had little to do with Dean's actual clientele, and more with the continued decline of general market conditions in the Atlanta-metro area. An economic downturn followed the boom of the middle and late eighties, caused in large part by financial institutions overinvesting in construction and development loans. By 1990, the number of banks extending the highest concentration of these types of lending had decreased by almost two-thirds, and over thirty of the banks failed all together. His firm's sales had held on respectably at the onset of the downslide, but when he was swept into a lawsuit involving a particular project and the associated lenders for the builders, Dean got out as best he could.

Once the diagnosis had come, Dean had tried to go into the office a few hours each day, wrapping things up, and found he spent most of his time completing seemingly unending insurance claims related to his new course of care. By the time they'd told Maggie and he was a few weeks into treatment, he didn't have the energy to go anymore anyway, so it now all seemed to have worked out for the best. Dean was impressed by Maggie's astute observation.

"I think you might be right," he answered. Dean remained pensive, realizing that he now faced medical bills for extensive treatments. While they had insurance that covered much of it, they already understood the uncovered parts threatened to reach enormous sums. Neither he nor Krista really had any idea how it would all work out at that point; their first step had to be concentrating on beating the disease, then they'd worry about how to finance the war.

"And you know what else I think, Daddy?" she asked. "I think we just have to trust God to somehow make you all better if the doctors need any help."

He took his daughter in his arms and hugged her until he lost all track of time. Tears flowed freely, and he didn't care. When he pulled back enough to see her precious face again, he stroked her hair and put his finger on the tip of the previously scrunched nose. "I think," he said, "that's *exactly* what we need to do."

Chapter 7

True friendship brings
sunshine to the shade,
and shade to the sunshine.

Thomas Burke

The fourth month into his chemo treatments, in the time ultimately leading up to the bone-marrow transplant, Dean again shared his progress with his best college buddy. Sam, it seemed, had reignited his passion for fly fishing in a big way, and he constantly gave Dean grief for fishing for tiny wild trout or larger "dough bellies" in the Georgia mountains.

If Jimmy represented Dean's closest, earliest childhood friend, then Sam Childers was the poster child for Dean's college years and beyond. Sharing that love of the outdoors and music, they had often fished and played golf together whenever they stole any free time. Sam had been the one who taught Dean to play the guitar, and Sam eventually moved back out West a few years after graduation. He'd gone back to the roots of his earliest childhood, finally settling in the Pacific Northwest, but he and Dean had nevertheless managed to stay in close touch.

Dean shared much with Sam, peeling back protective layers he used to shelter others from some of the gorier details of his treatment. Sam liked the fact Dean still felt comfortable letting his guard down a bit when they spoke, and did his best to balance true empathy with an ability to keep Dean riled and able to maintain his sense of humor.

After one particularly draining conversation, Sam said out of the blue, "You know, if for no other reason at all, you have to beat this thing so you can come out here for some *real* trout fishing."

"Yeah," Dean answered. "Okay, you're on."

Now, Dean was well aware of the fact that the Deschutes, near Sam's home in Oregon, is a world-famous steelhead fly fishing river. The reason, he had once read, was because its steelhead will actively come to the surface for a fly. This isn't the case with all steelhead rivers, which is one of the reasons that casting for these chrome ghosts is such a challenging undertaking.

Dean was anxious to embark on a new path, a new distraction, and he was especially happy to do so with his good friend. Sure, he'd used a fly rod a few times early in his childhood when he and his dad broke them out in the late spring to chase bass during the mayfly hatch. Not unlike most anglers in the South, Big Bob had owned a cheap fly rod designated solely for this purpose. The annual ritual usually lasted a couple of weeks, and involved prolific breeding on the part of the mayflies, which have an extremely short life cycle, and a greedy appetite for spent insects on the part of the bass. During the same time, the water temperature typically warmed enough to charge up the bream activity as well, and this only made for added entertainment with fly rod in hand.

He and Maggie shared their magic on the water on multiple occasions. Even Jimmy broke out a fly rod now and then.

But this new pursuit with a fly described by Sam held the promise of something not yet experienced. Sam, after all, had formally introduced him to the sport during their college days at Florida State University, where Dean enrolled after getting his act together following Big Bob's death. He'd gotten the final details settled for his mother and elected not to return to South Carolina. It turned out to be one of the best decisions he'd made, and Dean thrived in his new Northern Florida sanctuary. When he wasn't playing guitar in some dive trying to scrape together grocery money in tips, he and Sam hung out together, got into minor trouble together, and in general had the time of their lives.

True to form, Sam looked forward rather than back, and gave Dean something he could cling to, look forward to. Fly fishing gradually became a vicarious passion in the days, weeks, and months Dean was unable to leave the confines of his home. With no standard treatments offering more than a six- or eight-month extension to his "sentence," the radical chemo treatment seemed their only viable option. For twenty-one days at a time, he received nine different chemo drugs, four separate injections and five oral medications. After a mere seven days off, the whole gauntlet began again, a pattern he endured for nine excruciating months.

Fly fishing in its barest essence provided a means of escape. Watching episodes of "Walker's Cay Chronicles," "Fly Fishing America," and other ESPN fly-fishing shows vicariously transported Dean to places he could only then dream of visiting. When he was fitful, unable to sleep at three o'clock in the morning because of the side effects of his pharmacological cocktails, the hosts of these shows introduced him to interesting angling characters and brought him closer to other people and places he decided he might enjoy meeting one day. Being rather competitive by nature, Dean devoured any and all fly fishing information ravenously, and convinced himself it was something he might actually be able to do more seriously when his health allowed a return.

The sheer mechanics of the sport captivated Dean. Even onscreen, he relished the sounds of the water bubbling around the feet of the host on the show as he waded in a far-off famous river like the Gallatin or Madison in Montana. Other times, the rhythmic lap of the waves on the hull of a skiff slicing across a Bahamas flat soothed his frazzled nerves and took his mind off the present.

The inherent differences between spin fishing and fly fishing intrigued him, as well. The spin fishing he'd mastered early in his childhood involved using a cast to propel the weight of the lure, which in turn pulled the line off the reel and through the air. The exact opposite was true of casting a fly. The videos he watched and articles he read about fly casting technique described the imperative of using the weight and speed of the *line itself* to actually cast the fly. It was not a sport of speed, agility or strength (unless one chased 150 pound tarpon or 300 pound marlin!). Fly fishing seemed more a sport of timing and grace, a peaceful serenity in extraordinary outdoor cathedrals. The whole proposition more than intrigued Dean, and Sam's trip incentive increased his desire to beat his diagnosis swiftly and soundly. "When you're done messing around with all this stuff," Sam reminded him, "we're goin' to do some *real* fishing."

"Yeah, okay," Dean had replied, trying not to sound patronizing. "I already agreed to go."

"I mean it, Dean," Sam pressed. "Don't be a pain in my butt! Just hurry up and finish with all this stuff so we can go fishing again."

It meant a lot to Dean, now, trying to survive this ordeal, that Sam had not only stuck by him, but purposefully and intentionally gave him one more reason to look *beyond* his illness and treatments. In short stretches at least, Dean focused on television shows and magazines that transported him away from the medicine, the joint pain, the muscle aches, the mouth sores, the nausea, the skin rashes, and the sleepless nights. For him, fly fishing represented a glimmer of hope.

Chapter 8

A friend loveth at all times.

Proverbs 17:17

Dean read straight from the fly fishing outfitter's web site, intrigued and fascinated with each new fact he learned. Sam had pumped him so full of information about their upcoming trip that his head was swimming, and he had trouble keeping it all straight in his mind. Granted, Sam was the ultimate organizer; but when added to his "never-quite-got-past-my-hippie-stage" quality, this stream-of-consciousness side of Sam sometimes exhausted Dean.

He hated admitting that to himself. The Follower, the intentional Christian in him, understood and cherished the gift of Sam's friendship. Others Dean had considered truly good friends over the years had just drifted away after his diagnosis. He realized and acknowledged that dealing with another's suffering could take its toll on the strongest of relationships, and tried to keep a forgiving heart, but that proved difficult for the human side of Dean at times.

Sometimes, he found, dealing with a friend's problems simply proves to be too difficult. The result is less a sudden separation, not a huge fight or divorce, but more a gradual ebbing of contact, which ultimately contributes to the withering of the bond. It was not unlike what had happened the many times he'd forgotten to water Krista's plants over the years, he mused. The little suckers could hold on for quite a while, grabbing every last molecule of water from the soil, but eventually, if no more water came, they just withered and lost their ability to bloom.

"Hmphff," he blew through his lips. "Sounds a little bit like my faith these days too." Dean struggled with this realization for a few minutes. The trip of a lifetime was quickly turning into a stress-builder, try as he might to keep a light-hearted, carefree attitude about it all. Why? Sam had told Dean he'd take care of everything, and had stood beside, behind, and everywhere else through every turn on this convoluted journey of Dean's. *And now here I am*, he thought, *getting aggravated because Sam wants to make it the very best he can—for me, not for himself.*

He rubbed the back of his neck with his left hand while he picked up his Diet Coke with the other. Dean swung his chair around and looked out the window as he leaned back. "Boy, I can really be a jerk sometimes," he said to the walls, promising himself he would make a concerted effort to be more appreciative of Sam's friendship.

With a new perspective now easing into place, Dean allowed himself to get more excited about the trip. For Sam's sake, he needed to be informed, involved, and engaged, so he swiveled the chair back to face his computer and focused again on the website link Sam had sent him. He read on, his apprehension easing with each new detail of what the early autumn adventure would hold for them.

Most Deschutes anglers are concentrated in the lower river in search of steelhead. The water and air start to cool and the river is less appealing to rafters. The traffic on the upper river drops immediately. Trout become fatter and less cautious. This is the best time of year for a leisurely four- or five-day trip from Trout Creek to Harpum Flats.

From a geographical perspective, Dean might as well have been reading a travel log about Ancient Cyprus—in Greek, no less. He had no idea where any of these places were, but knew instantly he wanted to see them all! He reached for a swig of his drink, and continued scrolling with the mouse.

The colors in the canyon turn from brown and green to shades of amber. The nights turn cool and frost can greet the early morning angler. Water temperatures drop to the mid to low fifties. Levels remain stable. Trout feed heavily on caddis, small mayflies, stonefly nymphs and crayfish. Steelhead are distributed throughout the river as a bonus.

"A chance to catch trout and steelhead? Wow." He whistled. "Now we're talking!" Dean picked up the phone and dialed Sam's number from memory. While waiting through the rings, he scribbled a few notes. Sam recognized the number on his phone, and decided to answer in true Sam form.

"Sam's Flies and Lies!"

Dean played along, "Got any night crawlers?"

"Sure thing, smart aleck, anything for our customers. I'll have a shovel and a coffee can waiting on you when you get here." They both laughed a bit. "Please tell me you're not calling to cancel. You're okay, right? I mean, no setbacks or anything?"

"Right as rain," Dean replied. "And, feeling a lot better about this trip now, too."

"You mean you weren't before?" Sam quizzed. "What's up with *that*? Chemo turn you into a wuss or something?"

"Or something!" Dean boomed, a true from-the-gut laugh. When he caught his breath again he added, "And that's Mr. *Bald* Wuss to you, Knothead."

"Oh, yeah, sorry. I forgot to add that!" Sam laughed.

"No, Sam, I honestly was feeling a little overwhelmed for a while, but now I'm just ready to go!"

"How the heck could you be overwhelmed? I told you I'd take care of everything—every last detail. Man, Dean, you're worse than my wife some days!" Sam tried his best to sound exasperated, but was ultimately unsuccessful.

"Yeah, maybe," Dean retorted, "but *I'm* a better dancer."

They both cracked up, relieving a little tension. From there the conversation turned more tactical, since they were now down to the last couple of weeks of planning, and they talked of gear, tackle, and schedules for the travel itself.

"Okay then," Sam concluded, "sounds like we're really all set. Unless something comes up for one of us, I'll pick you up at the airport next Thursday."

Dean agreed, and promised to bring new pictures of Krista, Maggie, and Gus. He hung up the phone and just sat at his desk for a while. Mindlessly, he ran his thumb and forefinger down the length of his Diet Coke can, then twisted it a quarter turn, and repeated the motion. Little beads of sweat trickled down across the red letters and pooled on the coaster.

His thoughts turned to the reason for the trip itself. He'd made it, at least this far anyway. The trip he and Sam had pledged to take in the weeks preceding his bone marrow transplant was actually going to happen. It truly was a miracle.

"I'm telling you, Dean, you need something to look *forward* to," Sam had said, "and everyone knows I don't need any more excuses to go fishing, except that you coming to Oregon will be a real celebration."

They'd made a pact that very night that as soon as Dean finished his experimental protocol, made it through the transplant, and received the green light to travel from his doctors, one of the first things he'd do was make a bee-line for Oregon, the Deschutes, and a few days with his old friend.

Dean leaned back in the chair, momentarily lost in the memory, running his hands through the newly returning growth that he still did not recognize. He chuckled to himself as he thought of the night, earlier that week, when he'd gotten up to go to the bathroom. He'd caught a glimpse of himself in the mirror out of the corner of his eye, and almost scared himself back to death. In thirty-nine years, he'd never had jet black hair, and the post-chemo regrowth was taking some getting used to.

"All I need now is a sequined jumpsuit and I could start a new career," he said out loud. He stood and stretched one arm up and out, posing, cocking his head to the side, and curling is upper lip, "Thankya, thankya very much."

Oh, it felt good to laugh; felt good to be planning something farther than forty-eight hours in advance; felt good to know he'd made it far enough to be able to see Sam again. His hands went from the top of his head to his chest, where they intertwined as he bowed his head.

"Lord, You are so good," he began. "I'm thankful. And I'm ready. Ready to know whatever purpose You've got in store for me."

He paused as another thought crashed into his head, disturbing him, shaking him to his very core. *What would my prayer have been if this had not turned out so well?* He'd said numerous times either outcome, life or death, would be "great" because he'd either be a miracle or be with God, and neither really had a downside as far as he was concerned. The reality occurred to Dean now, however, that perhaps it was much easier to say this knowing he was the former of the two. But, he admitted, he'd also been the latter, and could honestly say he felt a complete peace in the knowledge of Who was really in control.

"*Thy* will be done," whispered Dean.

I'm One who keeps My promises, came the answer. *Hold on, Dean, the ride has just begun.*

Chapter 9

You see the ways the fisherman
Doth take
To catch the fish, what engines
doth he make?
Behold! How he engageth all his wits,
Also his snares, lines, hooks and nets.
Yet fish there be that neither
hook nor line
Nor snare nor net nor engine
can make thine;
They must be groped for and
be tickled, too,
Or they will not be chatch'd
whate're you do.

John Bunyan, The Pilgrim's Progress

As preparations for the big trip continued, Dean realized that he knew very little about steelhead fishing. Sam's enthusiasm proved contagious, but Dean also admitted that the trip promised less fun without self-education on the major points and techniques.

Practical almost to a fault, Dean considered his purchase of *Lefty's Little Library of Fly Fishing* one of his very best investments that year. The recovery to this point had taken over a *very long* two and a half years, and Dean used the excuse to treat himself a bit. The multivolume series offered practical and technical advice on fly fishing in general from the legendary Lefty Kreh himself. To the uninitiated, Kreh is to the sport of fly fishing what Palmer is to golf, what DiMaggio was to baseball. Bernard "Lefty" Kreh is a working man's man with palpably humble beginnings, a World War II veteran who rose to legendary status in the sport, both as a writer for his hometown newspaper in Baltimore, and as a celebrated angler. A huge part of his legacy is genuine desire to pass on his keen proficiency to enthusiastic entrants in the sport. The fact Lefty did so in such a colorful and entertaining way was an appreciated bonus.

In the pages of the collected works, Dean discovered an expanse of useful information, like what a blood knot was, how to tie it, and when to use it. Lefty also brought forth an array of other well-known experts who offered their own personal points of view on angling for various species, or using certain techniques. As Dean's fascination with the sport expanded and increased, he found himself pulling the books off the shelf repeatedly to brush up on a fly pattern, or in preparation of finding out a new technique for pursuing a particular type of fish.

Remembering a book on steelhead, Dean stood and crossed the hardwood den floor to the bookshelf. His fingers slowly walked across the spines as his eyes skimmed the titles—*Fly Fishing the Inshore Waters, Modern Fly Casting Method, Knots and Connections*, then, eureka! He read the title out loud, "*The Teeny Technique for Steelhead and Salmon.*"

Extracting his prize excitedly from its hiding place, Dean felt like a kid, poised to claim victory in the Pick Up Sticks world championships. "A-*ha*!" he almost giggled, and made his way back to his chair, clutching his treasure to his chest. *At last*, he thought, as he settled into reading material that in no way involved blood counts, research study findings, or a scan of any part of his body!

Laying the book on the table beside his favorite chair, Dean rounded the corner heading for the kitchen. He knew Krista expected her errands to take at least a couple of hours, maybe more. He grabbed the pitcher of tea from the fridge, poured a tall glass, and retreated to the den. Almost immediately, Dean became engrossed in the details of Teeny's techniques. He'd never considered himself an overly-technical angler, and from what he read, steelheading could well demand more from him than he was used to. So many varying factors ultimately contributed to success. He'd heard stories of friends who spent an entire week's vacation chasing the silver giants, heading back home skunked and defeated; or fishing their hearts out to land but one fish the entire trip.

Well, Dean thought, *I'm just blessed to be here and going on this trip at all. I won't be greedy by asking for perfect weather on top of encountering a bunch of fish.* Such was the nature of the lore.

How many stories described the travails of anglers braving abhorrent weather conditions in search of steelhead? Dean accepted that his chances greatly improved by preparing for the worst. He was used to it, really. This recent journey epitomized the concept—pray for the best, be prepared for the worst. He knew a steely faith needn't preclude practicality, and Dean firmly believed the common sense God gave him was a gift he was expected to use. And, as long as he didn't start to kid himself by thinking he could outsmart or out-plan God, he did pretty well. He felt certain that this was what continued to provide a feeling of calm in the midst of his recent storm.

So Dean read most of the afternoon, pausing every so often to jot a note or underline a passage. By the time the opening of the garage door heralded Krista's return, Dean felt reasonably armed, with information anyway, to tackle the trip with Sam. *Don't kid yourself, Moone,* Dean mused, *for years you read every issue of* Golf Digest *ever printed and never broke par!*

By the time Krista's efforts had dinner smelling really good in the kitchen, Dean fully understood at least a few basic tenets of steelheading according to Jim Teeny. The author acquiesced that while these somewhat fickle fish can be, and are, caught on surface dry flies, through various "skating" or "waking" techniques that involved dragging the fly across the surface of the water, the most effective tool came via sub-surface wet flies. This specific method imitated the natural life cycle of the insects, something Dean understood. According to Teeny, this method created the best possible odds for a successful trip by limiting the impact of conditions beyond the control of the angler, like weather. Beating odds, Dean knew from experience, was a good thing, so he identified even more with Teeny's ideas.

Dean laughed out loud about halfway down page eighteen. "Keep it simple, stupid…Ha!" Dean said, "Who knew Mr. Teeny wrote this book especially for me?" He continued reviewing other basic facts and jotted notes as he went, trying to keep it as simple as possible. He decided to spend little time on details related to where or why fish held in certain types of water, or which parts of the river were best to fish; they planned to fish with an experienced guide, which was really the only way to fish new water and truly enjoy it. Part of the guide's responsibilities would involve knowing the best places to take them, as well as the behavior patterns of the fish in those locations. No, Dean opted for a few more minutes dedicated to educating himself on things like the migration and life cycle of steelhead, so he wouldn't come across as a complete idiot.

Maintaining his focus on all things practical, Dean set his sights on four basic rules Teeny outlined in his book. As he read, he determined that three of the four realistically fell under the direction and knowledge of their guide—including determining exactly where on the watershed or tributary to fish, locating the fish in that water, and ultimately, the fly selection to entice the fish. The other rule, however, captured Dean's attention, and he knew this place demanded his time and attention. It verily determined whether he could actually seal the deal when the guide inevitably held up his end of the bargain. He must be able to present the fly in a manner a wary steelhead considered worthy of a strike. Steelhead in this setting, as Dean understood it, were disinclined to move more than short distances to feed. He would need to get his fly deep enough in the water column that it floated precisely past the nose of his quarry.

The next day, Dean again pondered the concept of steelhead feeding patterns. The intensity of the examination weighed heavily, and Dean couldn't shake an analogy from his mind. The way he saw it, Jesus and his disciples must have felt a lot like steelhead fishermen. Jesus challenged the men He found to put down their nets and follow Him, to become fishers of men. Did they have any idea, Dean wondered, what they were up against? He brought it back to a personal focus for his prayers that day. In Dean's perspective, the Christian walk with

God paralleled a steelhead's feeding pattern; if God's love is the fly, he thought, and we are the fish, it makes a lot of sense really...some just go get it, immediately. They are hungry and actively seek the word of God and its gifts.

Dean thought about this for a while, and the analogy was working for him—it fit with the way he was feeling, and he connected with the common thread that had been woven throughout his journey thus far. Others, he imagined, wait for it to be dangled right in front of their noses, presented in a way that must be "just-so" that the appeal sparks their appetite. It disheartened Dean to realize some would simply sit and watch the fly float by, refusing to take it at all.

Were they not hungry, he wondered, or was it just that what was presented to them lacked sufficient appeal? Perhaps an early bad experience left some reluctant to go after it again. This last thought disturbed him, sticking in his mind as he readied himself for bed, and sleep eluded him most of the night.

Chapter 10

I may have had a tough break,
but I have an awful lot to live for.

Lou Gehrig

The wheels of the 747 touched down on time. Dean marveled at the landscape, the high desert plains, and the mountains that seemed to stretch higher as the plane made its descent. The plane emptied, and he grabbed his carry-on luggage before climbing the jetway to the gate. For Dean, the look on Sam's face beat any scenery from the flight. In those days prior to September 11, 2001, friends and family could still meet passengers as they deplaned, and his friend's arms waved a wild greeting.

Sam's eyes twinkled, and he followed Dean to the point they could actually grab each other's hands and shake fiercely.

"Well, as I live and breathe! You made it!" Sam's voice boomed.

Dean gave his friend's shoulder a few firm pats after shaking his hand, then answered, "Yeah, and I'm living and breathing, too! We should be in for one helluva week!"

They both laughed, walking toward the baggage claim. After loading Dean's luggage into Sam's truck, the two climbed in and they headed for Sam's place. The entire forty-five minute drive was non-stop chatter, catching up on family news, Dean's health, and of course, the fishing plans. Once at Sam's house, they were greeted by Carol, Sam's wife, who threw open the door and jogged down the sidewalk with her arms waving, crying and yelling at the same time.

"Dean Moone!" she cried, and then launched into a string of comments. "Oh, get yourself in this house right *now*. Let me look at you. Oh, you look *great*. How's Krista? I bet Maggie is growing like a weed. How was the flight?" This went on for a couple of minutes, and then Carol finally had to come up for air. She stood in her living room, hands on her hips, and grinned at Dean. "So," she finished, "we're *really* glad you're here."

They all cracked up. For all they had been through the last couple of years, for all the time they'd been friends, through the tears and the heartache and all the frightening twists and turns, if anything had changed, it was imperceptible. They agreed things were indeed just as they had hoped.

After a fantastic meal with Sam and Carol, Dean retired to the guest room. A few items still needed to be transferred to other bags before he and Sam headed out the next morning, and though he didn't want to admit it to his friends, the trip had tired him. He yearned for a good night's sleep. The excitement of what lay ahead helped offset the aches in his muscles, but he also knew a dose of good rest was in order if he was to have the stamina needed for the next few days' fishing.

Morning broke, with aromas of coffee and bacon wafting to

Dean's room. He quickly showered, then brought his bags for the fishing outing to the kitchen, setting them by the door. He and Sam exchanged more details in abbreviated spurts, between slurps of coffee and mouthfuls of bacon and toast. It was as if the last three years had evaporated the moment Dean stepped off the plane.

They put the dishes away for Carol and loaded up the truck. By midday, their lines would sail through the air and land in the trophy waters of the Deschutes River, aching to pull out a trout or steelhead. Either way, the next four days held the promise of unforgettable memories for the two friends.

The pair arrived at the fly shop at the appointed time and followed the instructions given by the guides as last minute preparations came together for their trip. They soon embarked on one of America's most popular guided fly fishing adventures.

After the truck made its way to the put-in area, the anglers and their guide quickly set out upon the river. In the four days and three nights ahead, they would fish and camp on the majestic Deschutes. This tailwater fishery boasts great numbers of both wild redside rainbow trout and Columbia River steelhead, with the lower section offering incredible whitewater and towering basalt canyons. Dean and Sam's particular lower-river journey began below the Pelton Regulating Dam on the Warm Springs Indian Reservation. From there, the river flows fast and furious through the vast high desert and into the remote Deschutes River Canyon, eventually spilling into Maupin, almost forty miles downriver. Since fishing from a boat was prohibited on the Deschutes, they would float awhile, then anchor, wade and fish. Dean enjoyed wading, relishing the pull of the current on his legs and the gurgling sound the water made as it rushed past them. When they weren't fishing, the scenic landscape beguiled angler and guide alike.

The early steelhead, Dean quickly learned, come aggressively to the traditional wet fly and often rise to skating flies. The technique proved simultaneously fun and daunting. Skating a fly involved purposely creating "drag" on the fly, by letting the line pull against the natural flow of the current, so that it left a small wake just under the top film of the water. The intent of this was to imitate an emerging fly making its way to the surface. The things he'd read in Teeny's book splendidly unfolded before his eyes! His preparation provided a sense of relief now that Dean held his ground in the river, but each potential take made his heart turn a cartwheel.

Dean continually marveled at his surroundings, the vast expanse of water welcomed them, big and open. Each day, the mule boat, as it was known, went ahead of them to make camp for the night. Far from roughing it, they dined on gourmet meals at the river's edge, taking in the sunset over the towering cliffs. Dean, Sam, and Chuck, their fishing guide, all broke out their guitars, entertaining themselves until bed time. Sam joked he'd taught Dean all he knew about fly fishing *and* playing guitar, and everyone played along good naturedly.

The second night, one of the other guides, Tim, who stewarded the mule boat, asked about Dean's taste in music.

"Well," he told them, "I grew up a Southern boy, raised on the good classic Southern rock, you know, like Lynard Skynard, Allman Brothers and such, but I also like The Eagles and most other types of music." He finger picked a few bars of Stevie Ray Vaughan's *Texas Flood*, and said, "As long as the melody's good and the lyrics are decent,

I'm game."

The angling musicians quickly picked up where they had left off the night before, and the offerings soon grew quite diverse. A riverside jam session took flight, covering tunes by Muddy Waters, B.B. King and Buddy Guy in a blues stretch, to pretty passable renditions of both *Desperado* and *Orange Blossom Special.* A few good flat-picking offerings of old gospel standards like *I'll Fly Away* shone for part of the night, and the evening capped off with the Allman Brothers' *Midnight Rider.*

"I've got one more silver dollar," Dean sang, "but I'm not gonna let 'em catch me, no…not gonna let 'em catch the Midnight Rider."

The next day, beginning the final leg of their journey, Dean came to fully understand why the Lower Deschutes had gained such fame over the years. He and Sam fought some of the meanest wild rainbows they'd ever caught, the redsides showing no mercy to the angler on the other end of the line. Dean fought one particular specimen for over twelve minutes. Each time he reeled in line the fish turned and shook its head and ran back downstream, the reel screaming as line burned through the rod guides. The fight reminded him how connected and alive he felt when he fished, each dip in the rod alerting him to the trout on the end of the line.

He hollered downstream to Sam. "*Help*, I'm chained to a Winnebago headed South in January! There's no turning it around!"

Sam cackled. "If you lose that fish," he yelled, "I'm gonna smack you, and good!"

When he at last hoisted up the twenty-three inch beauty with both hands for a quick photo, the huge grin beneath the mustache did little justice to the enormity of glee inside him.

He carefully revived the fish in the cold current and gently let her go, watching as she swirled her tail and disappeared into the mottled green and brown of the river bottom. He stood up and arched his back stretching fatigued muscles, taking in the landscape. On this portion of the river, the intense vertical drop toward the Columbia River raised the canyon rim almost two thousand feet above the water's surface. The immensity of it invoked a sense of awe that humbled Dean, leaving him feeling immensely thankful.

The final day, the fishing turned a bit. The wind blew fiercely cold and brisk up the canyon, and the fish didn't seem active at all. Chuck explained that this was the kind of day that exemplified how steelhead fisherman earned their reputation of being undaunted journeymen, and more than a little hardheaded.

"Fortunately," he said, "the river consistently pumps out huge hatches of mayflies, stoneflies, caddisflies, and midges, and a lot of terrestrials. So, today just might be the day to dead-drift nymphs or swing some Soft Hackles their way."

While Chuck rigged their gear for the day, Dean and Sam spotted several birds and even an occasional otter. Though the wind was crisp, the coffee hit their bellies hot and strong, neither of them yet knowing this would be the day that exceeded their expectations for the entire trip.

Chuck explained he would again float them down a stretch and anchor the boat, so they could get out and wade. They worked their flies up and down deep runs, where the current churned, grabbing and driving their flies deep to where the fish lurked. On other sections, where shallower water tumbled over riffles, they cast upstream, drifting flies along the way. They stripped in short sections of line as they brought their flies back in to cast again and again. Each man whooped on a few strikes, but neither succeeded in landing a fish.

As they drifted through the canyon, the towering cliffs above them cast shadows, and other areas of the great basalt were brightened as if illuminated by spotlights. If the fishing never got any better, Dean thought, it really wouldn't matter—this was breathtakingly beautiful.

But, never forgetting it was a *fishing* trip, he and Sam fully intended to give it everything they had until the very last cast. Around the next bend, they caught sight of the mule boat and realized with great surprise that lunchtime was already closing in upon them. They chatted with Tim about the challenging fishing they'd experienced over the first half of the day. He worked quickly to wrap up lunch, as he knew they all were anxious to land a steelhead their last day on the river. They ate as quickly as their chef had prepared the offering, and bid Tim a heartfelt, but fast, farewell until dinner.

Jumping back in the boat after lunch, they floated the next stretch to a beach of sorts, off from which jutted a gravel shoal, and Sam and Dean again grabbed their rods with determination. They continued the waltz of the day, each casting, retrieving, and casting again. Dean made one particular cast and watched the line carefully as it swung through the deep pool at the end of the run. Nothing. As he started to strip back in, he grumbled. His line was caught on the rocks.

Just as he started to let out some slack, hoping to dislodge the fly, his line started to scream off the reel. The only thing that came to Dean's mind was that he had no idea what to do. What was he supposed to do? He'd never hooked anything like this before, not even what he'd likened to a vehicle earlier in the day. Chuck realized what was happening, and immediately came to Dean's side to coach him on landing the fish. It was a mostly technical oratory, with some yells and barks thrown in for good measure. Both of them knew this might well be the fish of a lifetime, both equally trying their best to make landing it a reality.

Several minutes later, the guide hoisted a huge steelhead in his net, with Dean laughing out loud through exhausted gasps for air. They exchanged high fives all-around after releasing the fish, and all sensed what the experience meant for Dean. It represented so much more than just landing an elusive trophy-sized steelhead. Hope. Redemption. Validation. Success!

Chapter 11

There are no great things,
only small things
done with great love.

Mother Teresa

As they drove back toward Sam's house for the flight home, Dean's mind swept back over the streamside conversation shared with his best friend earlier that morning. During a break in the action, Sam had asked Dean why he kept referring to his love of fly fishing as a metaphor for his faith. Dean hadn't consciously made the analogy, but he now realized the impact it had made on Sam. Numerous nights by the fire, as they all played guitars and laughed, subtle comments alerted Sam to a change in his friend. Sam had always been a pretty "grounded" guy, faithful, doing the right thing, but readily admitted he struggled to understand a daily walk of faith, a deeply personal relationship with God. He struggled to understand how his friend practically embraced the ordeal he'd survived.

Dean shrugged his shoulders out of habit, and then straightened his cap. His brow furrowed a bit as he tried to take the question seriously, in the manner he thought Sam had really intended. To begin with,

Dean hadn't consciously realized he regularly used such a metaphor; it just came naturally, like reaching into the refrigerator for the milk jug without stopping to contemplate a distinct like or dislike of dry cereal.

So he now attempted to ponder the emotion behind the analogy. What was it that continued to draw him to the water, to the challenge of hooking a fish on a fly? Why did the solitude of a small stream and the swirl and pull of the waters around his legs keep him so grounded, despite the current inner and outward turmoil of his life?

His mind retuned over and over again to a single word. Hope. The way Dean saw it, a fisherman returns to the water for another day simply because he has hope. Regardless of the level of success he encountered during his last outing, he has a renewed hope that this time is a fresh beginning. He arrives armed with knowledge acquired from previous outings; he possesses an unquenchable, seemingly irrational hope that today will be THE day to catch THE fish.

And so it goes—on and on—the dance not unlike the walk of faith. The promise of his personal faith, Dean held, did not automatically provide some mystical "get out of jail free" card. It didn't provide immunity against the experience of loss, grief, or pain. In fact, in the perspective of a refiner's fire, some people he knew held that the trials we endure make us stronger in our faith.

Now Dean readily admitted he was not this type of person. Even after the many struggles he'd endured throughout his life, he flatly refused to believe that God, his God, a loving and devoted God, purposely caused people to suffer simply for the sake of suffering. If he indeed subscribed to this view, then truly his whole belief of his rescue from the brink of death for a specific purpose no longer held water. No, a life of faith for Dean was not about being sheltered from every storm; it was about having a relationship with a God who would teach him how to dance in the rain.

Chapter 12

If I fished only to capture fish,
my fishing trips would have
ended long ago.

Zane Grey, Rivers of the Everglades

Dean remembered the experience, the questions from Sam and the wrestling he did with himself, a full eighteen years after that incredible trip with his dear friend—a trip that, merely in its planning and eventual occurrence, had changed his life in ways he still could not completely convey. He held on tightly to the love of his friend who encouraged him and pulled it all together, and still held onto where the journey brought him.

If nothing else, he fully realized he was an exception to the rule. He had defied the odds to survive the first experimental treatments he underwent. He had defied even *more* statistics to survive the bone marrow transplant back in those days. For nearly two decades, he had served daily as a living, breathing, walking testament to many that a terminal diagnosis could not only be survived, but further still, one could thrive and live an incredibly full and meaningful life.

He rebuilt his business, even more vibrant than before, and his life with Krista and Maggie gradually fell back into step. As he continued his recovery over the subsequent months and years following his Oregon adventure with Sam, he constantly met others who shared a common thread of connection through cancer.

A friend would mention her brother, or someone at church would mention a close friend's daughter who had just recently received this or that diagnosis. It seemed that, through Dean, others felt a higher level of comfort, inspired to share their stories and empowered to maintain their hope. Over and over, this effect revealed itself to Dean. One particular day, at a clinic checkup, he met a new friend.

Scott Wilson and Dean chatted a bit about the weather, the wonders of the clinic, the abilities of Dr. Richards, and the like when the conversation turned to Dean's journey. Many people, both patients and staff, at the clinic were aware of what Dean and Krista had endured almost twenty years ago. Theirs was not a relationship known for some espoused level of false perfection; rather, the couple's journey illustrated fierce commitment, to both each other and God, along with the validation that a truly successful marriage was based more on how it weathered life's storms rather than whether or not the inevitable storms occurred.

For some, the minor details weren't always accurate, but the general outcome of Dean's story rarely got lost in translation. Dean had survived much, and while he didn't just wear it out there on his sleeve for the world to see, he shared his experience when asked because he truly believed it mattered to those who did the asking.

"But if you're so okay," Scott asked that day, "then why are you here *today*?"

"Oh, that's just because Dr. Richards insists I come in for a checkup every six months, even when everything is going great," answered Dean. "I've gotta tell you, in this instance, I'm not gonna complain. Gray has become a great friend of mine and Krista's over the years. Honestly, if told me to come once a month I'd do it, if he thought I needed to."

Scott had just recently celebrated his return to "contact with the public" following his own transplant. A textbook "type A" personality, he'd wrestled fiercely with the reality of traveling the road that lay ahead, increasingly discouraged with the continued treatments and the projected time frame for recovery. His wife shared grave concerns with Krista in the waiting room. As wives sometimes do, the women bonded instantly through the family of cancer. Jane worried that Scott's attitude toward recovery would be just as critical to his survival as the treatments he'd undergone.

After visiting the clinic, Dean was of course aware of Scott's recent procedure. As was often the case, however, he was oblivious to the conversation between the two wives. So, as the two men discussed topics that moved from small talk to details of Dean's personal journey, Dean just did what he usually did. Naturally. He answered Scott's questions, told more details of his story as he was asked. At one point, he reminded Scott he was an eighteen-year survivor—not just of a diagnosis of cancer, but a *terminal* diagnosis.

Scott stared at Dean, and Dean could at once tell things were processing. He'd seen it before, and just waited. Finally he tried to bring Scott back around to their conversation.

"You okay, Scott?" Dean asked.

"Um, yeah," he replied quietly. "I guess when I'd heard people mention a little of your story before, I just didn't realize it was that long ago."

Dean smiled warmly. "Yep," he said, "it just so happens that you just had the modern version of the exact same transplant, for the exact same disease, I had—eighteen years ago."

As Dean's words sunk in, Scott's whole aura gradually, but visibly, changed. His body language eased. Sadness and tension perceptibly melted from his expression. To be clear, it wasn't as if he was literally or instantly transformed in dramatic fashion, but Dean had indeed experienced this before, and understood what happened. Whatever anyone chose to call it, one thing was very different for Scott as he left that office. For the first time in a year and a half, he had *hope*.

The next day, the phone rang. Krista answered.

"What did your husband say to my husband yesterday?" came from the other end of the line. No hello. No small talk. Krista knew what the call was about; she'd taken this type of call before.

Scott's wife shared with Krista the change in her husband. "You know, it's been really tough," she began. "The last few weeks, Scott's outlook has really digressed. Facing the fact that there was a real chance he might *not* beat this, well, it's been so hard." She paused to gather her composure. "When he came home from the clinic, I knew something about him was different. Please tell Dean, I don't know what he said, but I do know he and Scott were meant to run into each other yesterday."

"I'll tell him."

"Thank you."

Dean knew it, too. Over almost two decades, one constant

continued to surface, the fact that regardless of how he might try to muck it up on any given day, God's timing is perfect. Krista smiled, and handed the phone to him for a few more minutes of conversation.

"Dean," Scott's wife continued, "oh, I just don't know. I mean, he's been to the counselors, seen the doctors. It always seems like he's just doing it because he thinks it's what he's *supposed* to do. It drives him crazy, you know? He's such a dominant personality, a great businessman; he runs the show. This whole experience has left him feeling so out of control, so helpless."

"But today," she continued, "was different. The difference was you are *real*. You're not just someone he heard about, or read about, or saw on TV. He met you. Talked to you. Shook your hand. He knows now, I mean really believes, that it is possible to beat this."

Dean and Krista discussed several times over the next few days the conversation with Jane. Krista identified with her pain and frustration. Dean knew first-hand what Scott faced. They knew the power of their shared belief regarding such encounters; that a chance meeting at a restaurant, or even running into someone at the dry cleaners, was more providential than accidental. Regardless of where others fell in the spectrum of belief on that point, Dean carried the thought with him, and never missed a chance to share a kind or encouraging word. Somehow, he vehemently believed part of the reason he remained where he was hinged on his ability to be with people like Scott at the right time.

It makes all the difference, really, he wrote in his journal later that night, *this calling I feel to share my story. I'm not being egotistical. It's never been about me anyway. I've known that from the beginning, and believe it still. If I just had some operation, survived cancer and went on about my life, that would still be miraculous on its own. But if I'm not meant for more, then why am I still here?* He stared out the window, stroking his mustache before his pen met with paper again. *I can tell others are skeptical at times, wondering if the story I share is too "neat," too Pollyanna-ish, too much like a Frank Capra movie...but I know the truth. I also know the Truth, and it really IS that simple. I don't pretend to think I was saved "because of my faith." I've been a faithful follower of God's Word since I was a child, but I've seen others much more faithful than I lose a child, or a spouse, or their own lives. I refuse to live under the illusion that somehow my faith saved me. I'm rambling a bit tonight, eh? This, however, is what I do know...Because of what happened in that clearing, I know that my faith survives and thrives to this day because God has faith in me. Me. A mess. Me. His faith in me causes me to want to be a better follower, better person. It reminds me of a paraphrase of a conversation between C.S. Lewis and his wife, Joy Gresham, in a movie some years back. Joy asked him after he finished his prayers if he thought his prayers changed God. Lewis told her that wasn't the reason he prayed— "I don't pray because it changes God," he told her, "I pray because it changes me."*

As Dean closed his journal and moved it to its resting corner on his father's old desk, he knew in his heart the words he wrote were true, true to him. It aligned with his faith and with his gut, which told him a purposeful life didn't necessarily require a grand or high profile purpose. If he could share his story and bring one person peace, and somehow save another from one more sleepless night, and maybe prevent one more tear from falling, and know that just one more soul had a little more hope than before hearing Dean's story, well then, he thought, that indeed served a purpose he now felt blessed to fulfill.

Chapter 13

I still love to dwell upon what awaits me,
the plans I've made and
those yet to be made.
I find that looking backward
makes the looking forward
even more delicious.

William G. Tapply, Memory Jogging

As life slowly regained a semblance of normalcy and routine, Dean allowed himself to loosen his grip on his former cancer life. Weeks blended into months and gradually, as his survival time blended into years, he shifted from "survival" mode to making peace with his "survivor" label.

The financial quagmire left in the wake of the experimental treatments and subsequent bone marrow transplant provided a persistent, though thankfully, not insurmountable, irritation for their family. Dean's business rebounded well, thanks to the knack he had for maintaining and cultivating relationships. A deal here, or a venture there, provided an opportunity for him to gingerly re-engage, and laid a firm foundation for what grew to be a more successful, expanded version of his former company. He also found himself on a more even keel, noticing that situations or encounters that would have sent him over the edge a few years before now failed to even ruffle a feather.

Krista's teaching career continued to bring her joy and satisfaction, and allowed time for her to spend with Maggie as she hit her teenage years. They argued and bickered as mothers and daughters often did at that juncture, but Maggie never acted like a petulant child, and Krista did her best to not smother her blossoming girl.

Fortunately, over the years Maggie still enjoyed time at the cabin with her parents on the occasional weekend. Although Krista never caught the fishing fever, she welcomed the quiet days and peaceful setting. With all their family had endured, the atmosphere seemed more intimate, more comforting, than any other place on earth. Each possessed their own special connection to the cabin, but all relished time spent there together.

One particular June afternoon, Krista curled up on the porch swing, accompanied by the latest entry on her summer reading list and a cold glass of lemonade. She intently turned page after page, while Dean and Maggie readied their fly tackle. Dean's spirited love of fly fishing endured beyond his trip with Sam, and Maggie eagerly soaked up her father's enthusiasm. The conspiratorial duo snuck down the path, and arrived creekside full of muffled giggles. Dean pointed Maggie upstream, and turned to wade out toward a favorite riffle.

Maggie watched her father glide across an effusion of green shimmers. Her gaze held intently on the casting figure, taking in the ease of the back and forth motion of his rod as it sent the fly line sailing through the thick summer air. *I could watch you do that all day,* she thought to herself. The fishing days of her early childhood remained tucked in a special corner of her heart, but days such as this captivated her very soul. Months at a time had passed when she didn't dare entertain the hope of another day on the water with Dean, when his battles with such a vengeful and conniving enemy had consumed their entire lives and held them hostage for that moment in time.

She abruptly turned her lithe frame upstream, already-long legs stepping around smooth rocks and over the occasional log. The smile left by the image of Dean lingered, and she clung tight to that mental picture, letting it roll around in her mind. Finding her favorite pool, she began making casts toward the head of it, letting her fly sink with the tumbling current, swinging out as the pool emptied into a long, deep run. Maggie worked the section of water just as Dean had taught her, taking a step or two every few casts, landing her line as if she were ticking off the minute marks on a clock, waiting for any pause in the line, any change in direction of the drift, because either could signal an interested trout on the end of her line.

They whooped and hollered back and forth as the sun sank slowly behind towering short leaf pines.

"Daddy!" Maggie shrieked to her father. "Look at this one!"

"What a beauty!" Dean said as he moved toward her. He enthusiastically validated her catch, noting the size and colors of the trout, but careful not to patronize her in any way. "You've really gotten the hang of this, huh, Bugs?"

Maggie beamed. She removed the hook from the mouth of the fish, all by herself, and revived it before releasing it into the cool, clear water. Suddenly, she was overcome. A wave of emotion cascaded over her without warning, and she slumped onto a nearby rock, her shoulders shaking. She buried her face in her hands.

"Maggie?" Dean asked quietly, moving to her side. He hesitantly reached for her shoulder. "Bugs, come on, what's wrong?"

Her copper ponytail shook vehemently back and forth beneath her cap. Maggie couldn't find any words, and she knew looking at her father at that moment would only inflame her already fragile emotions. Several minutes passed before she regained her composure, and even then, her voice shook and her breath came in short spurts. "I'm… sorry…Daddy…" she gasped.

He gently swiped a piece of hair from her forehead and moved it behind her ear, letting his finger linger on her cheek. "Ahh, Maggie," he sighed, "sorry for what?"

She choked back sobs. *What's wrong with me?* She wondered. *I'm acting like I'm eight again!* Control eluded her. She sniffed. "Today's just been so amazing," she began. "The creek's awesome, and we actually caught fish…"

"And that's a reason to cry? I'm sorry, sweetie," he confessed. "I'm trying, but I'm not following you."

She shook her head again. "It's just that…" she caught her breath again, "some days are really normal, you know? We've gone back to our ordinary life."

Dean nodded.

Maggie shook her head. "In all the routine day-to-day stuff, I somehow never let myself imagine we'd do *this* again. It's been *so* long."

"But we've fished together before now, right?" Dean asked. "I mean, it's been a few years, and we've caught some good fish together since all the recovery stuff has been behind us."

"True," Maggie agreed. "And I honestly can't explain why today is different. When I let that trout go just now, I didn't want to. Like I said, I can't explain it, but I didn't want that moment to end." Maggie paused, searching for words that could verbalize her adolescent confusion to her father. "Daddy, I was *so* scared for *so* long." Silent tears slid down both cheeks. "But I didn't want to tell you or Mom because you had so many other things to worry about. Even after you were well again, there was your business to get going again, you know…just, *stuff*." She sniffed. "I don't know what it was about that fish, but I wanted to hold onto him and never let him go."

Realization crashed in on Dean. He and Krista thought they had gone to great lengths to protect Maggie during his treatment, transplant and subsequent recovery. While they were as honest with her as possible, they diligently refrained from having overly-intense conversations in her presence, and did what they could to shelter her from the ugly reality that existed in a battle for one's life.

Maggie, however, was no fool. Bright and vibrant, she possessed keen intuition and insight that provided her wisdom beyond her years. Now, even several years after Dean's recovery, the quality remained undiminished. Maggie's emotions hung on a ragged edge, raw and unabated, and her father knew he must listen and acknowledge all she was feeling now, in the creek, at his side.

"Oh, Daddy, I'm sorry," she whispered. "I don't know what's come over me."

"Take all the time you need, Bugs."

She smoothed her bangs to one side under the brim of her cap, and laid the fly rod across her lap. "I'm not sure why this is all surfacing *now*," she admitted. She was grasping for explanations to mature questions in an emerging adolescent mind, compounding her confusion. "It's weird. You've been better for a while. We know you've beaten it completely. Today was just…*perfect*." She looked up at him, hazel eyes swimming in fresh tears. "I guess I just want more days like this," she concluded softly. "That's all."

He pulled her close, rubbed the palm of his hand on her back, and raising the brim of her hat, kissed her forehead. "Maggie." His voice came out hoarse, barely audible. "I can't imagine what all of that did to you. It's a lot for a grown up to go through, much less," he caught himself here and didn't say "a child" but chose his words carefully, "someone with less life experience. If I could change anything about what happened to me, it would be to take away any pain my sickness caused you."

She knit her brow, wrinkling her nose as she'd done since about age three. Dean could tell she wanted to ask another question, but he didn't press her. She examined the trees, the rocks, the creek bottom. Suddenly, she looked him straight in the eye. Her father had always accepted blunt questions, and met them, to the best of his ability, with honest answers. "Dad," she said, "is it okay that sometimes I'm still scared?"

"What do you mean, *still scared*?"

Maggie exhaled an exasperated sigh. "You're well now. At least as far as we know. I mean, it's been, like, seven or eight years since you got sick." She paused. "I don't know. I don't want to be all worried or anything, but, I *am* worried. Some days, I'm just afraid, like out of the blue, that something else will happen."

He softened. Now, he understood. "Oh, Maggie...my dear, sweet, Maggie."

"What?"

"I know it may not make sense to you right now, but I just can't worry anymore," he said.

She shifted on the log. "I don't know what you mean."

"Honey, I accepted a long time ago that *I'm* really not the one in control. I can't imagine you'll completely understand this for a long time, but personally, I arrived at a particular kind of peace when I was sick." He struggled to craft the words into something his daughter would understand as the very nexus of his faith. "A lot of people call it the 'peace that passes understanding' and for me, I guess that's pretty accurate."

She nodded. "Daddy?" she asked a final time.

"What, Bugs?"

"Do you ever wonder why you got sick?"

Again, he answered honestly. "Sometimes, yes," he said. "Or at least, I did when it was all happening."

"Do you think it was some kind of a test?"

He thought for a minute. "No," he shook his head. "I really don't. I think I tried to focus on asking questions like 'why now' or 'why this' instead of 'why me'. It's just kinda the way I'm put together."

"Then, okay. I have another question. Why did *you* live when other people die?"

Oh, to retain the transparency of youth, he thought. *No hidden agendas, no underlying plot. Just blunt, let-it-all-hang-out words for all to hear.* "Maggie," he admitted, "I have no idea."

She swirled her feet in the water, concentrating on the rings of ripples her wading boots left in the creek. "So, you're saying you think it's all just…random?"

Dean laughed. "Wow!" he exclaimed. "You're full of questions today, huh?"

Maggie shrugged. "I guess so."

"I'm not sure I'd say it's all 'random.' The way I look at it, situations and outcomes seem random to us because we don't understand the way things work together much outside the confines of our own lives. Does that make sense?"

"Sorta."

"You don't sound convinced."

Her tears threatened to return. "I'm just trying to figure out, how do I *not* worry? I'm sorry, Daddy," she said. "Sometimes I'm terrified I'll come home from school one day and you'll be sick again."

He pulled her close, kissing her forehead again. "I can't promise you anything, honey," he admitted. "But, let me ask you a question now."

She closed one eye, and looked at him sideways. "Uh, okay."

"Do you know *anyone* who can predict the future?"

She shook her head.

"Okay," he continued. "And, even if someone *could* predict it, do you know anyone who could *change* what was going to happen just because they knew it beforehand?"

Again, the same response. "No."

"Right. So, the point I'm trying to make, Bugs, is *nobody* knows what will happen. Not next year. Not next week. Heck, not even twenty minutes from now."

"Um, Dad, that really doesn't make me feel a lot better," Maggie admitted.

Dean smiled, his expression softening. "What I'm saying is every day is a gift. We shouldn't waste our time worrying about what might happen. I know that sounds impossible, and I'll admit it takes practice, even sheer minute-by-minute determination some days. But, honey," he paused, lifting her chin to look at her, "I've learned I can't control *what* happens, only how *I* react to it, how *I* deal with it."

As if something had bitten her on her backside, Maggie jumped up from her perch. The way a teenager's mind worked still completely baffled Dean on most occasions, and he eyed his daughter closely to see what would happen next. She suddenly grabbed her fly rod, and pointed it towards the next run in the creek.

"How much more time are you gonna waste sitting here answering so many questions?" she asked indignantly, hands on her hips.

Dean blinked, perplexed, and stared at his daughter. "Is this a trick question?" he asked. "Because you oughta know I'll sit here all day if you have more things you want to ask."

She rolled her eyes. "Nope," she said. "No tricks." She waded downstream a bit, and called over her shoulder. "Just make a note, Dad, that I'm *agreeing* with you. I don't want to waste what's left of the afternoon crying and worrying anymore."

Dean watched as an amazing woman-girl moved farther down

the creek. He shook his head, bewildered by how quickly her moods could change, but also grateful for their conversation.

Maggie called to him, "You gonna just stand there and let me catch all the fish?"

"Not on your life!" he howled back. He was pulling fly line back through the guides as he stepped through riffles when Maggie's line went tight.

She let out a whoop, and squealed, "Fish on, Dad! You've got some catchin' up to do."

"Indeed!" he replied, and cast across the run, watching his fly sink into a liquid kaleidoscope.

Chapter 14

Too many of us, when we accomplish
what we set out to do,
exclaim, "See what I have done!"
instead of saying,
"See where I have been led."

Henry Ford

A full decade later, still keeping with his every-six-month-checkup regimen, Dean arrived ten minutes early for his appointment with Dr. Richards, and perched himself on one of the waiting room chairs. This last round of respiratory infection had proved stubborn, and though Dean had encountered many bouts with such things over the last fifteen years or so, he felt compelled to check it out. Since his bone marrow transplant (BMT), he'd been admitted to the hospital ten times over twenty years with such infections—once with pneumonia, once with strep pneumonia, and another four with early pneumonia—so it wasn't like he didn't know the drill. But something seemed different this time. He felt more tired.

"Mr. Moone," called the nurse from the door, "Dr. Richards will see you now."

Dean pushed himself from the chair and followed her to the exam room. He listed his various symptoms, their duration and severity, and answered a few of the nurse's other questions, watching as she typed all the details into a laptop computer.

"Okay, Mr. Moone," she drawled, "given your history with these infections, we're gonna go ahead and run a CBC to save you some time and so Dr. Richards will have that info when he comes in."

Dean nodded.

"Celia will be back in a jif to poke you some more. The doctor shouldn't be far behind," she called over her shoulder.

As predicted, Celia promptly flew into the room to gather what she needed in a whirlwind and darted back out. Within fifteen minutes, Dr. Richards tapped twice on the exam room door and pushed it open. He reached out to shake Dean's hand.

"Dean," he said, "nice to see you again. Though I must admit," he continued, "not under these circumstances." Over the years following Dean's transplant, Gray Richards had grown to be a great friend. He and his wife spent time socially with Dean and Krista, and Dean thought the world of him. The feeling was mutual.

"I'll agree with you there, Gray," chimed Dean. "But, I figured I'd better mention it when I first got here—just can't seem to shake it."

Time had graced Gray Richards gently. He looked much the same as he had when Dean first came to see him, save a little more gray at the temples and a few more laugh lines around his soft blue eyes. Those eyes scanned the laptop screen to gather a few more details. Dean sat, waiting and wondering. When Dr. Richards took off his glasses, he looked straight at Dean.

"I can't believe I'm saying this to you," he began, "but Dean, I don't like what I'm seeing in your bloodwork. Even for an upper respiratory infection, the counts aren't where I'd like them to be, and a couple of them are just really out of whack."

Dean ran his hand through his hair and arched his neck and rolled his head in a circle. "How out of whack are we talking, Gray?" His brain immediately went where the doctor suspected. "Are we talking, like, 'oh man, we're gonna have to stick your butt in the hospital again,' or are we talking something else?"

Gray pushed his lips together and flopped his stethoscope back around his neck. "I want to run some other tests," he said, "and send a couple of them to a special genetic lab. I think, however, that your marrow is failing again."

Dean felt like someone had kicked him in the stomach. Sweat broke out across his forehead, and he felt nauseated. Dr. Richard's words swirled in his head—*I think your marrow is failing again*. Oh, God.

Once Dean regained a little composure, Dr. Richards went over a few more details with him. He planned to send Dean's current results straight to the genetic lab, and had his nurse call ahead to alert them that they would be sending them over. "I'm not going to let you wait to find out about this if at all possible, Dean," he explained. "I can only imagine what a shock this is to you."

As promised, the genetic lab results came back quickly. Dr. Richards' office called to set up an appointment, and Dean returned to the clinic. When he heard his name called, he experienced a feeling of déjà vu, mingled with a heaping dose of dread.

Dr. Richards came in the exam room and gave Dean a firm pat on the shoulder. "Dean," he began, "I know you're a no-nonsense kind of guy, so I'm gonna shoot it to you straight."

"Okay," Dean replied. He looked up at his doctor and friend, and squinted. "I'm not going to like this, am I?"

"Nope," the doctor answered, shaking his head as he sat on his stool, "and I don't like it one bit myself. It's such a rare occurrence I had to ask them to test it again. Dean," he paused to take a deep breath, "my initial tests confirm what we suspected. You marrow is indeed failing again."

Dean swallowed hard and let his eyes move all around the room, taking in everything, in slow motion. It all seemed so surreal—like an episode of the Twilight Zone. He shook his head as if to chase away the cobwebs, and turned to look at his doctor. "So, what—exactly—does that mean?"

"For now, it means we try to get this respiratory infection cleared up, and we'll make a game plan for the other part of this in the meantime."

Dean appreciated the man's honesty. Some doctors he'd run across in the last two decades since his first diagnosis of non-Hodgkin's lymphoma gave explanations with a condescending presumption that the patient knew little about their own bodies, health, or protocols for their proposed care. Dr. Richards was his friend, someone who also knew this wasn't Dean's first rodeo. He never spoke intentionally over his head, and was open and honest with everything related to Dean's treatment and care. "Let's let the antibiotics run their course for a few days, Dean," said Dr. Richards. "And we'll set you up to come back in after next Thursday."

And with that, Dean headed back home. His head reeled. Bits of phrases floated through his mind…*marrow failing again…wait a week…we'll know what we're dealing with*. Could it be? Dean prayed, hard, all the way home, trying not to let his fears run away with him. If he learned nothing else during his first journey, he knew that fretting over "what if" brought only more distress. Prayers flowed for patience. For peace. For discernment. For no more bad news. Dean knew Who was still in charge, but he also acknowledged his own humanness, and at that moment, he admitted honestly and openly, that the human in him absolutely did not want to be sick again.

Chapter 15

It's like déjà vu, all over again.

Yogi Berra

Almost nineteen years after a life-changing conversation in a room full of Barbie dolls, Dean sat in his den awaiting the arrival of his now grown-up Maggie. Earlier in the week she had accepted her parents' dinner invitation for the weekend. He'd prayed most of the day. Krista and he had held each other and cried. They had prayed together. He looked through old photo albums, smiling particularly at the ones capturing the many fishing trips they'd enjoyed together since that day at Nantootla Creek. He felt tired.

How do you do this? He'd asked himself that question hundreds of times in the past week. How do you tell your child you have cancer? Again! He'd read the Psalms all morning, clinging to the 147:3 verse promising, *He heals the brokenhearted and binds up their wounds.* He admitted feeling brokenhearted. He wrestled with God's timing. God's plans. Dean's purpose.

All he could keep coming back to was the thought, the reality, that he'd done all this before. He'd been sick before, and had been given an unthinkable prognosis before, and even died before, and then he'd beat it all—defying every single set of odds that existed. Almost.

He fought with himself, resisting the temptation to be angry with God. The truth was that he really wasn't angry. The emotions that felt the closest in the days following the final test results were sadness, disappointment, longing, and a twinge of what he could only call dread. He truly had no doubt that the disease could be defeated again, and he knew this because he had already beaten it once. It wasn't about not trusting God to deliver him a second time from the jaws of death, for if anyone believed this possible, it was Dean.

No, what sat so heavy upon his heart was the knowledge of what must come next. Defeating the monster he faced yet again would require all their courage, all their strength, all their faith, and even then, a healthy sprinkling of miracles along the way. He couldn't escape feeling like the rug had been pulled from beneath him. In the years following his survival of the first journey he felt he'd served God's purpose for him, that he had continued to live a life that gave others hope and peace. So now, was it normal, he wondered, to feel confused? What would the purpose be this time? Or was there one?

Dean, do you trust Me?

The sound came from a small whisper deep within Dean's heart. He recognized it, though he tried to shut it out at first. It came again, asking something slightly different from the first question.

Will you trust Me?

Oh, Lord, Dean thought. I really do. I know I put myself through a lot of unnecessary stress and pain when I refuse to trust You. I really make a mess of things when I think I'm in charge!

My time, My ways—remember? But, you're forgetting something, Dean. Scholars over the world debate it regularly. They have since ancient times, and they will until there are no longer any scholars.

Dean was confused. "What are we talking about?"

This is no personal attack. You don't need to ask "why me?" Not every bad thing that happens in the world occurs because I somehow allow it. Forces are at work that quite simply no man will ever be able to comprehend.

Dean put his head in his hands. "Then what do I do now, Lord?"

Answer the question. Will you trust me?

"Yes."

The quick knock on the door alerted Dean and Krista to Maggie's arrival. She felt weird knocking on the door to the home she grew up in, but somehow it seemed rude to her to just barge right in on her parents.

"Mom, Dad, it's me," she called from the foyer. "Hey, where are y'all?"

"In here, Buga Bear," said Dean, "in the den." He rose to meet her halfway, enveloping her in a big hug.

"Hey, Daddy." She loved the fact that Dean still used his pet name for her, even though she was in her mid-twenties.

"Hey, yourself," he said. "How's school life going? Is your group of kids still working out as well as you thought?"

Maggie sat on the sofa as her mother entered the room. "Oh, yeah. They're *great*. I think it's going to be a good year."

She'd followed her mother's lead and gone into teaching,

although Maggie felt a pull toward special education. She loved her students, and felt like her work somehow made a difference in their lives.

"Hey, Mom," she said casually. Krista had walked to the couch to kiss her daughter on the cheek and give her a hug. "Something sure smells good in there," she added.

"It's coming along," her mom replied. "We'll eat in an hour or so if that's alright with everyone."

"So," Maggie said, "I really appreciate the invite and all, but it was kinda out of the blue. Not that I don't see you pretty regularly, but I get the feeling something's up."

Dean and Krista looked at each other and back at Maggie.

"What *is* up?" she asked.

Dean cleared his throat before speaking. "Maggie, I can't believe I'm telling you this," he began, "and I'm still not sure I know how to tell you this...."

Maggie's eyes widened, and she could feel her pulse racing in her neck. "Dad, whatever it is, can you just please tell me? You're scaring me."

"Well, your mom and I are scared, too, Bugs," he said. "Seems I have cancer again."

"WHAT??" Maggie surprised herself by the volume and pitch of her remark. "But, how? When? You don't just have a metastasis almost twenty years later!" She reeled off a myriad of questions to the point that Dean and Krista just let her go for a while before trying to answer. "Is it something new? What are you going to do?"

While Maggie asked her questions, Krista walked back over

to the couch and sat next to her. They'd tried to raise Maggie without too much sheltering or protectiveness, and knew she'd come to expect honest, frank discussions with her parents. She was now a grown woman, but still their daughter. It was a difficult dynamic to negotiate for all of them as the conversation unfolded. Krista reached for Maggie's hand as Dean started answering her questions.

"Okay, let's take this one step at a time," he said.

"Okay." She let out a ragged breath.

"So, the reality of the situation is that my bone marrow is failing again. This time it's at a genetic level. The doctors think it may be partially a result of some of the treatments from my first go-round." He paused, letting this initial news sink in before continuing. "What that means is this isn't a metastasis or a new type of cancer, like a tumor or something."

"And…?" Maggie asked.

"And," Dean said, "we've talked with all my doctors, had all the right tests, the whole enchilada. As it stands right now, we have two choices."

"Which are—what?" she asked.

"One, do nothing. Or, two, consider another bone marrow transplant."

"*Another* transplant?" Maggie gasped. "Dad, are you serious?"

"I sure wish I wasn't Bugs, but yeah, I'm serious."

"So," she said, "what now?"

"We've talked about it, prayed about it, cried about it, and talked about it some more, but we also want you to weigh in. Bottom line is my plan is to go for it, Maggie. I can't imagine, since I'm only fifty-six, throwing my hands up and saying, 'I'm done.'"

"Absolutely, you're not done!" she replied. "And, we're all in this together!"

Maggie turned her head to look at Krista. "Mom?"

When she spoke, Krista's voice was raspy, but firm. "Honey, I completely agree with you. I just wish somehow your dad didn't have to endure this again." She paused. "That we all didn't."

They continued the dialogue, outlining all the details. When Maggie asked if the risks were greater with a second transplant, Dean explained what he knew from talking with the doctors. Many of the drugs they used were the same, but the way they used them differed; they gave them in a different order, different doses, and improved the offset of some of the worst side effects, especially the nausea. He also explained what he called the "babysitting factor," the reliance he would have on people to stay with him, drive him everywhere, and so on.

"Those types of things you probably don't remember from the first time this happened, but we'll all need a lot of support to get through this, logistically, in addition to the emotional and spiritual sides."

Maggie's mind raced. School had just started, for her and her mother. She had applied to several graduate schools and would try to secure teaching jobs near them when she learned of acceptances. Her townhouse was on the market. And now this? *Lord, help me*, she thought. *Help us all.*

Chapter 16

This is what it is to be loved,
and to know that the Promise was
when everything fell, we'd be held.

Natalie Grant, Held

The second time around, the ease and convenience of technological advances like email communicated news to friends and family quickly and efficiently. Dean found he used this method of updating regularly as he reluctantly embarked on his second journey.

He sat down one afternoon to email Sam. This would be the second-most difficult conversation, after the one he had already had with Krista and Maggie, and he used the "It's a guy thing" excuse to email rather than call this time. If he had been completely honest with himself, Dean would have admitted that he was terrified he'd break down like a baby if he called Sam on the phone.

Given the fact that they were already planning another big fishing adventure for the following summer, Dean knew he had to shoot straight with Sam—as straight as he could anyway, given the unpredictability of what he was about to endure. He grabbed a Diet

Coke out of the fridge on the way to the computer. Closing the door behind him, he sat down in the dark green leather chair and stared at the screen. His arms felt like he'd just done two hundred bicep curls, and he knew he was stalling for time. After taking another big gulp from the can, Dean ran both hands through the hair he would again be losing, breathing in deeply and exhaling only after he could hold his breath no longer.

He moved the mouse to Sam's email address in his directory and double clicked. In the subject line he decided to type, "May need to reschedule the trip to Henry's Fork." He began with the usual small talk, updates on Krista and Maggie, and mentioned the real reason he'd sent the email was so Sam would know there might be a chance they'd have to put off their trip of a lifetime to the famed Henry's Fork of the Snake River in southern Idaho.

Once he'd gotten that far, Dean surprised himself by being very factual and concise in relating his latest news. The bottom line was he still knew Who was really in the driver's seat, and He'd already gotten Dean past this disease once. There was no reason to think this time would be any different. Was there?

After all, unlike the first time, another BMT didn't mean another cancer, and if it were possible, his faith was even deeper and stronger now than it had been the first leg of the journey almost two decades earlier. And so he continued:

In the last few weeks, it has been determined that my bone marrow is in the process of failing. It has been severely damaged at the DNA and genetic level by all the previous chemo, radiation, and infections. Although fairly common within a few months to a few years after a bone marrow transplant, it is very unusual for this to happen so far removed (18 years) from the transplant. So far, it has just affected my platelets—red and white blood counts are still pretty good. There is no fixing or repairing, due to the fact it is damaged at this level. At some point in the future, which is pretty unpredictable, another BMT will be my only option. Most likely would be in the next 6 to 18 months.

Dean added some follow-up comments about staying in touch, sent his love to Sam's wife, Carol, and said he'd call soon. Then he read back over what he'd written to Sam, and clicked "send."

Without any warning, he was suddenly overcome. The shock, resentment, doubt, and fear that had accompanied the events of the past few days reached a crescendo Dean could not withstand. He crumpled forward and put his head on his forearms atop his father's beat-up oak desk.

"Oh, Lord," he choked through sobs. "Why? Why now? Why this—*again*?" He was scared. Utterly petrified. It's one thing to be afraid of the "unknown," to know it's something that will be bad but not really understand how bad, all the gory details. For Dean, this was another thing entirely. He knew what he was about to endure. He really *had* been through it before. As much as he wanted to beat this again, his apprehension was greater because he knew what he was up against.

The mere thought of repeating what lay in the dark shadows of his mind brought beads of sweat to his forehead. He vividly remembered the searing pain in his muscles from the chemo, and the way radiation therapy made everything taste horribly metallic, when he could taste at all. Images flooded back to the time he vomited so violently he had burst several blood vessels in his eyes.

"I look like the Son of Satan," he'd told Jimmy over the phone. "Around my eyes I look like I've been beaten up, and the whites, well, let's just say there isn't any white to be seen right now."

He remembered the sensation of feeling like he would spontaneously combust from the inside, with hot flashes that came on suddenly, soaking his clothes; the next moment, he'd be freezing with chills. And then another memory rushed back. A day when he remained hospitalized after his first bone marrow transplant, so sick, so exhausted from the unending ordeal he actually contemplated suicide. *I might have seriously considered it,* he wrote later in his journal. *I was so tired, so beaten, so helplessly ill, and the life insurance I had would have served Krista and Maggie a lot better than the medical bills that continued to grow.*

Dean remembered most, however, that the humor miraculously embedded in that particular situation was that he was too sick and too exhausted to act on his thoughts. *I'd kill myself,* he wrote, *but it would just take too much effort at this point.*

Yes, he knew all of this and more. And he didn't want to be here again. Dean knew he was feeling sorry for himself, but at that moment he didn't care. He also knew he needed to continue to pray. Pray hard, openly and honestly. He already knew there was nothing he could not say to God. This was not the time for ambiguous, "please be with me" prayers. Dean needed to express the range of all he was bearing, and then, he knew, he must turn it over and let it go.

"When we spoke in the clearing all those years ago, You said there was more work to be done. More work! How do You expect me to finish the work You intend if I'm sick again?" He rose from the desk and was pacing now, like he did when he was trying to solve the *Times* Sunday crossword puzzles, hands on top of his head.

"Haven't I done it?" he asked, throwing his hands into the air. "The talks, the lectures, the meetings, the personal and private conversations with troubled souls facing the same journey—*all* of it? I can even accept maybe there's something else *I* need to learn here, but why put Krista and Maggie through this again? I'm trying, but I just don't understand."

He collapsed into the chair, laying his head back against the worn, cool leather. Closing his eyes, Dean concentrated on his breathing, his fingers traced the carved oak trim at the ends of the chair arms, back and forth, as if polishing the wood. He felt the hot tears continue to skate down his cheeks, but made no effort to wipe them. *Just breathe. Breathe. In. Out.*

Oh, damn it all, he thought. Opening his eyes, he turned the bright blue fullness of them upward.

"Lord," he spoke aloud, "*help* me. I don't know what to do. I have no doubt that *You* know. Please, I need You to lead me to Your will, bring me peace." He whispered the word again, "Peace."

That's better. I'm here, Dean. I never leave you.

"Am I dead again? Because I don't usually hear You—I mean really hear You."

No, you're not dead again. Let's go for a walk.

Dean pushed himself out of the chair and downed what was

left of his drink before opening the door. He rounded the corner of the hallway and cut through the breakfast area to go out through the French doors. Pausing on the patio, he took in a deep breath. The air was warm and light since the oppression and humidity of summer had passed, and the sun warmed his face. Stepping onto the grass, he headed for the garden path. As he reached the edge of the path, a breeze came up, and he could swear the sun brightened a bit. Immediately, Dean recalled the sensation.

"Are You laughing at me?" he asked. "After all this time, I do at least know You have a pretty good sense of humor."

No, Dean. Laughing at the joy you bring to me.

"Beg your pardon?"

You are, you know—such a joy. You walk in My name on days most people would curse Me over and over. Your faith is contagious.

Dean kept walking, enjoying the feeling of the breeze against his skin.

I won't answer your questions, Dean. Not today. Not all of them.

Dean stopped walking. He knew God knew all the things he'd been thinking as he moved along the path. Still, he was disappointed he would not get the answers he so desperately wanted.

Not all of them, but I will answer the biggest one: not this time. Not now. This disease will not defeat your spirit, nor cut short the time of your earthly life. Again, I will deliver you; again, for a purpose.

Dean began to weep openly. He had stumbled so much during the past weeks; had questioned his situation, his very faith. He had questioned even the personal devotion of his sovereign Lord, who now, embodied in his garden, had laid all Dean's fears to rest. He wept, for his fear, for his doubt, for his guilt.

"Please forgive me, Lord. I can't believe how short I still fall—every day. It must disappoint You terribly."

You're human, Dean. Believing in My promises doesn't mean you won't stumble. Do you remember when I told you to just chill out—in the clearing?

"Of course."

What I meant was, quit trying to be perfect all the time. Quit feeling so obligated. My love is here. It's always been here. Your choice is to accept it, and you have. Now, you must continue to give love as I have loved you. It really is that simple.

As the wind started up again, Dean knew his conversation was drawing to a close. This was not the time for grandstanding or more questions.

All he could manage was, "Thank you."

And thank you, Dean.

When he returned to the house, Dean went back to his study and took his Bible off the table. After spending some time in the midst of several of his favorite passages, a calm settled over him, and decided to start dinner before Krista came home.

Chapter 17

Life is a journey of the heart
that requires the mind,
not the other way around.

John Eldredge, Desire

The next several weeks blurred into each other. Each day brought a new test or preparation for the ultimate goal of undergoing the transplant. For this second journey, the doctors told Dean early on that chemo or treatment alone would not get him where he needed to be, wouldn't save him. This second bone marrow transplant remained his only option.

He and Jimmy met at Martha's Café for coffee on several occasions in the weeks that followed, and rather than talk about the impending procedures, their conversations held promise of springtime fishing and more fun days together on the water.

"You know," Jimmy said, "'bout the time you're able to get out and about again, those bass up at the lake oughta be hitting some topwater action."

Dean smiled. "Yep. Sounds like something we need to plan

on."

"Right!" Jim chimed in agreement.

"You know, it won't be long before they'll isolate me again," Dean blurted one morning. "As we get closer to the transplant date you're gonna have to deliver the coffee instead of me coming here."

"Yeah, okay," Jimmy said, "but just don't expect me to make you biscuits!"

Dean laughed.

"That's where I draw the line."

As time drew nearer to the scheduled procedure date, Dean felt bombarded. Attacked by an Enemy. Physically. Spiritually. Just as his mind absorbed a new situation, it changed, or an additional dimension for which he felt utterly unprepared inconsiderately inserted itself to the mix. As at peace as he was with Who remained in charge of his situation, Dean found discouragement creeping in, tugging forcefully, unrelentingly, at the corners of his cloak of faithfulness.

He maintained his usual sense of humor when sending out his email updates, and tried to also share the reality of their needs, as well. Dean knew canned or sugar-coated representations were unnecessary, maybe even insulting to his prayer warriors, but he found it very difficult to be totally transparent. He did, however, constantly thank his friends for their tenacity in supporting his family.

Jimmy dropped by one Tuesday afternoon with some fishing magazines, and they caught up a little.

"So, you know your emails don't fool me, right?" Jimmy said.

Dean knew Jim was attempting to lighten him up a bit, but he just felt too tired for the usual banter. "What?"

"C'mon, Dean," he said. "You're too good to all of us. I know you don't sugar coat everything, but we can handle it if it's not all rosy all the time."

Dean sighed. He stared at the ceiling, and then closed his eyes. "You're right, Jim," he admitted. "Or, at least a little anyway." He kneaded the heel of his palm on his forehead, feeling exhausted. "I just figure a lot of people might get tired of hearing about a new medicine, or some other tests I had to have done, or how many times I threw up yesterday…Whatever." He added, "Oh! I actually did fall asleep with my head in the toilet yesterday though!" He said, "I was so exhausted from throwing up I just couldn't move. Now *that's* a little new and exciting."

"Man, you're selling a lot of us short," Jim said, irritated. "You don't have to be on a cake walk for us to walk with you, you know?"

"Yeah, not with you I don't," Dean answered. "I know that. But I'm not sure about others. A lot of people don't know what to say to me as it is, or what to do with themselves when they're around me. So, yes, maybe some days I make it out to be a little less severe than it really is."

Jimmy nodded. "I get it."

"I'm just ready to have a conversation with someone that doesn't center on an appointment time, a drug therapy regimen, or blood counts. I still have no doubt, and I mean *no doubt*, that we'll beat this. I'm just ready to have it happen a little more quickly."

Jim laughed, "Ha! Yeah, that old Moone patience you're so famous for!"

"Don't you mean *infamous*?" Dean chortled. "I don't know,

Jim. It just seems like every time we get *this* close," he held up his thumb and forefinger, squeezing the space between them smaller, "to making real progress, something else changes. I'd just like to be able to keep moving ahead for an extended period of time."

They visited a while longer, discussing Falcons football and what the upcoming season held for the Braves. Dean promised to start hounding his doctor about how soon he would be able to start fishing again following the transplant.

"Ok," said Jimmy, standing to head for the door, "so, I'll see you."

Dean's mood eased following his friend's visit, but still the attacks seemed relentless. In the following weeks, as many times as Dean shared a story about how awesome God's presence in his journey was, the Enemy would throw another curve ball and skew the situation. Just the previous week, a mild respiratory infection advanced to pneumonia, which took two rounds of antibiotics and steroids to conquer. His blood counts, however, remained unaffected enough to continue moving toward the ultimate goal of the transplant. This being the second time around, he and Krista both struggled with the enormity of the task at hand. Just keeping track of the appointments and medications alone proved exhausting.

An illustration of how all-encompassing the journey had become occurred in late November. Their thirtieth wedding anniversary celebration consisted of an entire day at the doctor's office, soaking up yet again more education and preparation details for the upcoming procedures. Both of them moved from nurse, to tech, and back to nurse, each passing hour overwhelming them incrementally.

Information specific to Dean's situation also became more clear and detailed by the hour. While much remained the same, an equal amount had changed regarding procedures and processes in the realm of bone marrow transplants in the past two decades.

"Okay, Mr. Moone," said the nurse seated across from him, "you understand how critical it will be for you to isolate yourself from any groups or crowds, right?" Her name tag read, "Laurie Dumant, R.N." Her auburn hair held a few strategic streaks of silver, but framed her porcelain skin well, highlighting the sparkle in her green eyes. "So, just to be clear, that means no restaurants, no stores, no going to church, and avoiding pretty much anywhere more than three people gather… for a minimum of six months."

Dean well remembered the drill from the first BMT, but verbalization of the time frame blindsided him. He'd been so sick the first time around that his memory must have tricked him into believing it had not been more than a couple of months, a semblance of "euphoric recall." *Surely not six.* He sighed. "Six months, huh?" he whistled. "Wow."

Nurse Dumant simply nodded, and continued, "Right, six months. And no driving either." She talked and signed papers at the same time, making stacks for Dean and Krista as she covered each topic. "No traveling out of state until further notice, and you'll need to have a transportation plan in place, since you'll be coming to the hospital daily for a while. You can't be left alone during this time." She paused, letting Dean's mind catch up to her checklist.

"Right," Dean said, "got it." His mind raced, and he couldn't help feeling discouraged. Six months. 'Round the clock babysitters.

Joy.

Krista's meetings progressed similarly, though hers focused on how to administer the expanding number of medicines Dean would need, how to keep up with critical information they must monitor, and militant germ-prevention protocol. They left the hospital lost in their own thoughts, saying little on the ride back home.

When they finally retired for the evening, Dean pulled Krista close to him. She laid her head on his shoulder, both of them exhausted and weighed down with the events of the day.

"Happy anniversary," Dean whispered as he closed his eyes.

"You too," said Krista, smiling through silent tears. "I love you."

She dropped into a fitful sleep. The date of the procedure was set on the calendar, and this was shaping up to be one holiday season none of them would soon forget.

Chapter 18

The Lord has promised good to me;
His will my hope secures.

John Newton, Amazing Grace

On the fifth of December, Dean sent one of his email updates to his faithful friends. True to form, it contained the usual humor, but also acknowledged the enormity of the task at hand.

Greetings everyone. You are cordially invited to join Krista and me for a wonderful and exciting New Year's Eve celebration. This year, we have decided to go to Northside Hospital for a bone marrow transplant and hope you will join us in spirit.

He went on to lay out the specific schedule of placement of the central line, outpatient chemo, and the like. *Just think*, the email read, *chemo for Christmas and a bone marrow transplant for New Year's Eve—there's gotta be a song in there somewhere!*

While Dean and Krista both longed to get the transplant done, each time they received definitive plans, the reality of everything came crashing back on top of them. They agreed it already seemed like a pretty long journey, and they were just at the beginning.

A couple of weeks later, Dean began to feel some of the effects of the journey he did not so fondly remember from the first BMT. His mouth had the anticipated metallic taste in it all the time, and mouthwash or toothpaste only made it worse. Though Dean had joked about having a weight problem since he was a baby, the bloating and puffiness of his body gave clues to the effects of the two high-dose steroids he took. Much of the day he felt like he'd consumed seven or eight pots of coffee at a time, making any sleep beyond fitful cat naps impossible, which in turn made him cranky. He apologized daily for inadvertently stepping on Krista's toes; he knew he was far from a good patient. He was too tired and sick some days to realize just how bad it was, but sometimes knowing he was being a jerk only made him feel angrier with himself, which in turn caused him to act badly. It was a vicious cycle, to say the least.

"Can I get you anything?" Krista asked.

"No."

"Do you need another blanket?"

"No."

"How about the pain? Do you need another dose?"

"I'm good."

Krista checked the central line and the chart they used to track all the meds. "Okay, so I'll check on you later, then. Oh," she added, "I'm running out later. Do you want me to pick you up a new fishing magazine or something?"

"I'm *fine*," he snapped. "How about if you just do whatever you need to do, and I'll let you know if I need something?" Dean regretted the words as soon as they escaped his lips, but Krista bit her tongue. If she had learned anything from the first time around, she knew that her husband was a bad patient. He despised being waited on, and he couldn't stand answering all the same questions over and over again. Unfortunately, a sizeable portion of the questions had to be asked daily. The steroids made him want to climb the walls, but most days he just felt sick and tired of feeling sick and tired. Though she intuitively knew all this, his gruffness could still take her by surprise on occasion. After much prayer spread over two decades, her current approach was to respond with humor, and a touch of aloofness, until the spell passed.

"Have it your way, *mule head*," she called over her shoulder. "You'd just better hope for *your* sake I'm not out for a mani-pedi when you decide you do want something!" And with that, she made her exit by firmly closing the door to the den.

Chapter 19

It is not good for man to be alone.

Genesis 2:18

Three decades earlier, on a late March weekend, a friend of a friend had set Dean up on a blind date. His friend and accountant was Mike Schell. Mike's wife Lisa had a best friend named Cathy, who taught elementary school. They all wanted to set Dean up with one of the other teachers at Cathy's school. Dean had met Krista Banks briefly at a school PTO picnic at some previous point, so they were both mildly aware of who the other was. That was as far as it went.

Dean had lived at Mike and Lisa's house for about three weeks the previous year—waiting for the apartment he wanted to become available. He and the couple got to know each other a little better, and Dean was grateful for the space. Based on that experience, he trusted their judgment of character and thought the idea of a blind date sounded pretty good to him.

The next Saturday, after bringing himself to a standard he considered "looking decent," in his opinion at least, Dean hopped in his truck around 5 p.m. to go pick up Krista. The round trip spanned over 150 miles, given that they lived in suburbs on opposite sides of

Atlanta. The loveliness of spring jumped out at Dean during the drive, with bursts of azaleas and dogwoods around every corner. The scenery put him in a relaxed mood for the evening.

Promptly at 6:30, Dean knocked. Krista swung the door open with a warm greeting. He noted to himself how casually the woman before him radiated classic beauty; the fact she seemed unaffected by this trait only enhanced it. Her warm smile told Dean right away that she was someone who laughed easily and made others comfortable. Any remaining apprehension about the blind date aspect of the evening slipped from his mind as he joined Krista on the porch swing.

After some small talk, they headed to the restaurant for dinner. Over appetizers, they naturally began the expected casual conversation, talking about work, hobbies, family, and the like. At one point in the conversation, however, the course of the exchange inadvertently turned.

Krista popped a last bite of potato skin in her mouth and wiped her fingers on her napkin. "So," she said, "your dad's a dentist, right?"

Dean looked up from adding another lemon wedge to his iced tea, surprised. "Um, actually," he replied, "he *was* a dentist. My dad passed away about five years ago." He picked up the teaspoon and gave the contents of the glass a stir.

Krista looked surprised. "No, he didn't," she said, unconvinced. "Lisa said your dad is a dentist in Atlanta."

"Well," chuckled Dean, "then we put someone who looked a lot like him in that box!"

Krista was mortified and at a loss for words. She tried to stammer an apology, but Dean stopped her. He laid the teaspoon back down on the table and smoothed the tablecloth. They both sat and looked at each other for what seemed like a long time, and then Dean burst out laughing. Krista exhaled loudly and joined in the giggling.

When Cathy had set them up, Krista was under the impression that Lisa knew Dean fairly well. But Lisa didn't. It turned out that Cathy really only knew what she had heard from Lisa, which was mostly a combination of hearsay, speculation, and vague inference.

Dean was also under the impression that Lisa knew Krista pretty well. But she didn't. Lisa only knew her from the brief encounters Cathy related from school, but somehow Cathy had also talked Krista into being her roommate for a short time.

After having a great laugh over the whole situation, Dean and Krista relaxed, continuing their conversation. They talked about everything under the sun, and continued on the drive back to Krista's.

Instant attraction was obvious to them both, and Dean left Krista's apartment feeling the disappointment of having already made plans for the following weekend. He wanted to see her again.

The next day, Dean called Krista.

"Well, hello!" came the answer on the other end of the line when Krista realized it was Dean.

"Hi, yourself," he said. "I had a great time last night."

"Me, too. Even after I put my foot in my mouth, dinner was delicious!"

Dean laughed. They chatted for about five minutes or so, and then he made sure he got to the point before he missed his chance.

"Listen, Krista," he began, "I'm afraid I've already committed to something this weekend, but I'd really like to see you again."

"And?" she asked. He couldn't see her twirling her chestnut hair around her finger as she waited for his response. Krista knew already the feeling was very mutual.

"How about us catching a movie together—next weekend?" he asked, then quickly added, "whatever you want to see."

Krista didn't have to think about her answer, but she hesitated just a moment for effect.

"Okay," she said. "Pick me up at six, and we'll just see what our options are when we get there."

Dean hung up the phone feeling like he'd just discovered he had won the lottery. He didn't want to scare her off, but Dean felt certain after that conversation that his search for a soul mate had come to an end.

Another couple of movies and dinners, minus awkward conversation, only fueled the fire they both felt. With each date, it took longer to say goodnight. The week after that, Dean decided on a bold move, taking Krista and his mom to the Easter Service at their local church. And with that, Dean knew, after their third date, he planned to ask Krista to marry him.

Something told him she would likely accept, though for appearances he decided to wait a little longer before popping the question. When he'd waited as long as he could, on a glorious late afternoon in June, Dean took Krista to one of their favorite local seafood restaurants. It wasn't fancy, but Dean knew what he had planned for the evening; taking her somewhere else would tip his hand and let her know something was brewing.

They enjoyed a nice dinner, full of their usual laughter and conversation. The ride home proved a little quiet, but Dean was too lost in his own thoughts to notice. By the time they made it back to Krista's apartment, he was in his own world; he'd rehearsed the whole thing in his mind repeatedly, but he needed to stay focused, to make it perfect.

Krista's roommate had returned to the apartment by the time she and Dean arrived, so after exchanging a few pleasantries, they retreated to Krista's room. Seated on the bed, Dean dove straight into his rehearsed monologue.

"Krista, you have to know the last few months have been really, really wonderful," he began.

Dean continued for several minutes, but Krista barely heard the words. *He's breaking up with me*, was all she could think. *I've known I loved him since our third date, and he's breaking up with me!* She tried to maintain her composure but with an increasing degree of difficulty. Krista breathed in and settled her gaze on Dean's face.

"So," he took her hand as he neared his conclusion. "Because of all that, and so much more, Krista, will you marry me?"

Shock. Stunned surprise. Speechless.

"*WHAT*?" she screamed. "What did you just ask me?" Krista offered no opportunity for Dean to answer the question.

"Are you *serious*?" she was floored. Krista jumped up and danced around the room, squealing with delight.

Dean finally calmed her down enough to get her attention.

"Krista!"

She froze. "What?"

"Don't you want your ring?" He held out the ring that rested in his palm the entire duration of his proposal.

Through joyous tears she came toward Dean, hugging and kissing him.

"You better believe it, mister."

Krista spent the next twenty minutes trying to reach her family to share the good news. Since no one knew what a cell phone was at that time, she just kept calling until she reached an aunt. If she didn't tell someone, she knew she would burst.

After a call to his mother, who already knew what he had planned, Dean called his two best friends in the world. The first call was to Sam, and then he dialed Jimmy's number.

Both conversations were short and to the point, "Okay, man, get ready—you're gonna have to rent a tux!"

Dean and Krista married eight months after that first blind date. On their honeymoon, they both asked when the other had known they would spend their lives together.

"When you didn't run screaming and in tears from the restaurant on our first date, I was hooked," Dean confessed.

Krista feigned shocked indignation, "You're kidding!"

"Nope," Dean chuckled, "that deer-in-the-headlights look you got when I told you my dad died when I was in college…you were so *cute*."

"Oh *puh-leez*!"

He continued. "Seriously, anyone with that much grace was awesome in *my* book." Dean gave her leg a squeeze, "still is."

"Yeah, okay," she giggled, "if you say so."

"Okay," Dean said, "what about you? When did you know?"

Krista wrapped a strand of hair around her finger and caught Dean's profile out of the corner of her eye. She gave him a playful grin, leaning forward.

"Let's just say any man who would take a new girlfriend to church with his mom on Easter was awesome in *my* book."

"Really?"

She nodded. "I was very impressed. You knew what mattered to you, and you weren't afraid for anyone else to know." The strand of hair dropped from her fingers and landed on her shoulder. "It was refreshing."

"Well," he smirked, acting amazed. "Whaddya know?"

"Oh, and come here," Krista brought him back to the present, their honeymoon. "I'll only give you about fifty or sixty more years to keep impressing me."

Chapter 20

Take away all my sadness,
fill my heart with gladness,
ease my troubles
that's what you do.

Van Morrison, Have I Told You Lately?

Seven months after the second bone marrow transplant, Dean and Krista returned home on a Saturday, following Dean's five weeks in the hospital fighting graft-versus-host disease (GVHD). Neither was prepared for the adventure awaiting them. A mere three days earlier, conversations with doctors had convinced them both to plan on the stay extending at least another two or three weeks. The next morning, however, Dr. Richards floored them with new news.

"Dean, I think you just need to plan on going home Saturday," he said.

Dean and Krista exchanged shocked glances. This news felt out of character for the doctor, and though it brought excitement, both knew Dean was still very sick and weak, and panic coursed through their veins.

"So," said Krista, "you really think he's *ready* to go home?"

Dr. Richards chewed on his bottom lip and stared at Dean's chart. "I think," he said, "that you've both spent too much time here. We can teach you a few things in the next couple of days to make the transition smoother."

He noticed the look of terror on Krista's face. Dean had lost nearly seventy pounds, thanks to the muscle-eating steroids, the GVHD effects, and the fact that what little nutrition he *could* get came in liquid form from a fourteen pound bag he had to lug around at all times.

"You'll both be *fine*."

The next couple of days—filled with multiple lessons for Krista —passed more quickly than any had in weeks. Nurses and various specialized techs walked her through tutorials on attaching rubber tubing to a computerized pump that dispensed Dean's many medicines. She needed to learn how to flush the line, attach it to Dean's main pic line, or port, and how to add his meds to the IV bag. A separate second pump served to deliver liquid nutrition, since the GVHD affected Dean's GI tract so fiercely. A big eating day for him at that point was being able to keep down two or three teaspoons of solid food, so he depended on the IV sustenance for the time being.

Krista's emotions and mental-absorption capacity reached their limits by mid-morning on Saturday. She found herself very near a complete breakdown by the afternoon. Her usual calm and steely determination slowly disintegrated, and the unraveling infuriated her even further.

"I can-*not* do this!" she said, her words tense and quiet. Huge tears pooled at the edges of her lower lids, silently crawling over her lashes before sliding down her cheeks. Krista slumped in the chair, and she sat staring at her shoes.

The compassionate nurse demonstrated unwavering patience. "Mrs. Moone," she said, reaching for her hand, "I understand this is a whole lot of new information for you in a very short time. We all just want what's best for Mr. Dean. Please, can you to try just one more time?" The nurse patted Krista's hand, and then added, "You're really doing great."

"I'm used to teaching other people how to do things," she said. "This is all pretty foreign to me." Krista lowered her head and finally verbalized her worst fear. "What if I do something wrong?" she whispered. She looked up at the nurse, meeting her steady gaze. "What if I forget one of these steps? I've tried to do everything in my power to help keep him alive for almost *twenty years*...if one thing isn't done right, I'm afraid...I'll kill him." She buried her face in her hands.

There, she'd said it. She was a teacher, and a darn good one, but nursing was simply not her vocation. A natural caregiver, of course. A stoic force most people considered on the even keel. Krista rarely backed down from a challenge—but this was no ordinary challenge; her husband's life literally depended on her mastery of one afternoon's tutorial.

Of course, everyone wanted Dean to beat his latest challenge. As usual, making friends came easily to him, and his casual manner created an almost "drop in whenever you can" atmosphere in his room. This included hospital staff as well as his friends, and Dean realized quickly he'd unknowingly recruited his own private cheerleading squad, simply by being himself.

He'd spent hours talking with one of the orderlies about fly fishing on "The Hooch," or the Chattahoochee River, to non-anglers. Kevin White had grown up in the Atlanta suburbs, and shared many childhood adventures with his uncle on the Hooch, chasing fish—and time away from an unbearable home life.

"When Uncle Jay and I stepped into that ice-cold water," Kevin shared with Dean one afternoon, "I had a new perspective every time." He smiled at the memory.

"Yeah," Dean replied, nodding. "I know exactly what you mean."

Kevin continued. "Wading in the water, feeling the gravel under my feet…well, let's just say I've always felt like I was on a lot more solid ground in a river than at home." He adjusted Dean's pillow for him and then rested his hands on the rail of the bed. "'Course, you can't wade the Hooch very deep or for too long. Water temp's too cold, you know?"

Dean agreed. He knew at an average year round temperature of less than fifty degrees, that river wasn't conducive to wading without the proper gear.

"We didn't have waders back then," Kevin continued, "so we always took Uncle Jay's canoe with us…got out to wade the shoals when we wanted to, then floated down some more."

"Sounds like something I'd *much* rather be doing right now," Dean said with a slight chuckle.

"Oh, man," Kevin apologized. "I'm sorry, Mr. Moone. Listen to me going on and on. And you're here, just listening to me ramble."

Dean reached to put his hand on Kevin's forearm. "Kevin, are you kidding?" he asked. "I don't have many people to talk fly fishing with in this place. The doctors fly in and back out pretty quick, and after over thirty years of marriage, Krista will listen to me blab about anything for a while. But, since she doesn't fly fish herself, I know it probably gets old after the first, oh, two minutes or so."

Kevin laughed. Talking with Dean felt so easy, so comfortable. Kevin had learned through his work at Northside Hospital that some people just had that gift. Simply being with them offered easy conversation that flowed naturally between fast friends. What he had heard of Dean's story over the last month or so intrigued him. Though his shift officially ended before he entered room 370 that day, Kevin thought it might be helpful to Dean, and Krista for that matter, for him to stick around a little while.

"So what is it for you?" Kevin asked.

"Come again?"

"The fly fishing. You said the other day something about how it 'saved' you. You mind me asking what you meant by that?"

Dean smiled. "Careful, Kevin," he said, "you get me talking about fishing, and you'll be stuck up here *all day*!" He added, "But, it sure does take my mind off other things."

"You're saving me from an afternoon of errands and summer re-runs," Kevin laughed. "Please, I'd really like to know more."

Dean imparted what he called the "CliffsNotes" version of his journey, from the first bone marrow transplant to the present. "After the first BMT," he explained, "all the different drugs made sleep a fleeting thing. I mean, I was on, like, seventeen different meds at one point or another, sometimes as many as ten all at once."

Kevin just nodded, following the conversation and understanding all of Dean's explanations, given his years of work in the oncology wing.

"So, anyway," Dean continued, "my normal sleep pattern was, like, two hours of sleep, three awake. *Horrible.* I survived by watching all the outdoor shows on TV. They show some cool reruns at four in the morning, you know?"

"Yep."

"Well, I'd been a golfer in my earlier days, but lost my touch when I was so sick. I couldn't stand to not play well anymore, so I sorta gave it up. I stumbled on one of those fly-fishing shows in the wee hours one Saturday morning. 'Walkers Cay Chronicles,' I think."

"Oh, yeah," said Kevin. "Flip Pallot—that guy's a fishing magician."

"Right! That's the one. Well," Dean went on, "I was mesmerized. The whole thing just kinda sucked me in. Here I was, sick as a dog, not knowing if any of the drugs would work, up to my eyeballs in debt. You know, back then, even though I had great insurance, my out-of-pocket expenses tapped us out. I think it only took maybe six weeks to deplete twelve years of savings."

Kevin let out a whistle.

"I'm not saying that for effect," Dean said. "It's just reality. To understand what it means to me now, you kinda have to know where I was when I found fly fishing. Like I said, it was just, um…"

Kevin loved how Dean jumped from the main topic to ensure his listener understood every nuance of the story; it made them more fun to follow.

"What was I saying?" Dean asked.

"You were mesmerized," Kevin prompted.

"Right. So, here I was, stuck in a simply miserable pattern, and all these shows transported me to beautiful, exotic places; they introduced me to new species of fish—well, ones I never saw up in the little creeks around Dahlonega anyway."

"For sure," Kevin agreed.

"I ate it up. Started looking forward to the new shows, and especially liked the ones that taught you stuff. 'Use this weight rod and this type of fly when you go after these monster fish,' stuff like that. I decided *that* was something I could do. I started planning how I'd go here and there once I got myself back to normal. My best friend, Sam, planned a trip for us out in Oregon, where he lives, to fish for steelhead on the Deschutes. Every time Krista went out I'd ask for magazines or books on fly fishing. Drove her nuts, I think."

"You don't do many things halfway do you, Mr. Moone?" Kevin asked, amused, but certainly not mocking the amazing man before him.

Dean laughed long and hard. "Guess not," he answered. "Nope, not ever, really. But one thing you have to understand is what fly fishing gave me." He paused a minute, searching for the right words. "*Hope*," he said. "It gave me hope, just like I've been given throughout this entire journey. Now *that* hope comes from God, but so does what I get outta my fly fishing, I suppose—hope that there's something more to look forward to, some promise that extends beyond the confines of a hospital bed. It's that connection you mentioned earlier." He motioned to Kevin. "You remember when you talked about the gravel under your feet with your Uncle Jay?"

Kevin nodded. Now *he* was the one who was mesmerized.

"When I'm fly fishing, I'm *alive*. The crunch of gravel under my feet, the way the current squeezes and hugs my legs when I'm wading, the waxy, smooth feel of the fly line gliding over my fingers when I release it with the final forward cast...all of it...I'm *connected*.

"I get it."

Dean was on a roll, like a kid telling his Christmas list to Santa Claus. "Oh, man, but then—*then*! That moment when a fish decides it's your fly it wants to eat. Well, talk about feeling alive, connected! Something on the other end of that line is alive, giving it all they've got. And then, you let it go—release it to fight another day. I don't imagine a non-angler would understand, would they?"

Kevin raised his eyebrows, considering Dean's question. "Oh, I don't know," he said, "the way you explain it, I think just about anyone would understand what it means to you. It's pretty cool."

Dean decided to go one step further. He sensed somehow Kevin needed to hear the whole story.

"You know, Kevin," Dean said, "I could use that fly fishing analogy to explain my own personal journey of faith, too."

Kevin's eyebrows pushed together now, skeptical, but open to discussion.

"Don't worry, son," Dean teased, "I'm not *preaching* here—believe me. What I want you to understand is my story's kinda like the one I just described about fishing."

"In what way?" asked Kevin. "I'm afraid you just lost me, Mr. Moone."

Like so many conversations over many other years, the words fell into place and everything clicked. Dean himself understood it all more clearly than ever before. "Kevin, I'm sort of a catch-and-release story myself."

Kevin smiled.

"I knew when I beat this thing the first time around I still had work left to do. Sometimes it's as easy as having a great time talking with a friend, like now."

Kevin smiled again, looking at his folded hands on his lap.

"Other times, it's struggling through phone calls or gut-wrenching conversations. I've sat with parents who've just lost a child. Talked on the phone for hours with another who's just learned they themselves have cancer."

"Boy," said Kevin. "That must be tough to do. I mean, I help take care of people once they get *here*, but what you're talking about is something altogether different."

Dean nodded. "I remember one man," shared Dean, "whose teenage daughter had been diagnosed with cancer. I'd never met him personally, but we had a mutual friend." Dean paused to ensure Kevin was following his story. "So, somehow, it ended up the gentleman called me. I was always reluctant to just call someone out of the blue in situations like that. I usually gave them *my* number and left the offer open."

Kevin's head bobbed his agreement as he sat back in his chair.

"So, anyway," Dean continued, "we talked a long time, about things you'd expect, doctors and medicines, and also about other things, like how to search out some sort of peace during such a horrific storm.

I identified so much with him; I have a special place in my heart for daughters," he smiled, nodding to the picture of Krista and Maggie on the nightstand by his bed.

"Did she get better?" Kevin asked hesitantly.

Dean closed his eyes tightly, then reopened them. "No, Kevin," he said matter of factly. "She died." He took a deep breath. "It broke my heart. I had no words for any of it. No one could ever begin to understand why someone like that dies; why does someone like me have their life spared while a young girl with her whole life before her wastes into nothing?"

Kevin's exhale and ensuing silence conveyed his response.

"But, I'll tell you what *did* happen," Dean said. "And what I know to be true because of it."

"What's that?"

"The next day, her father called and thanked me. *Thanked* me!"

Kevin's surprise showed. "For what?"

"I asked him the same thing," admitted Dean. "And he said, 'for helping us believe this is not all there is.'" Dean stared at Kevin. "Is that unbelievable or what? They had been so engulfed in their grief, just from the diagnosis alone, they were absolutely paralyzed for weeks. None of them seemed to know where to move away from it or how to begin to get there."

"But you showed them," Kevin added.

Dean shook his head. "No," he said. "*God* showed them. I just helped them get their lenses focused a little better to see it."

They sat in silence for a few minutes, each lost in their own thoughts. Dean spoke first. "I went to her funeral," he blurted.

"Really?"

"Yep. I felt somehow I needed to. I shook her father's hand. It was the first and only time we met face to face."

The stories throughout the years all held different details, and each was deeply moving in its own way. Somehow, Dean's revealed purpose became offering comfort to others making a journey down the path he'd previously traveled. He never patronized, never trivialized, and most definitely never tried to ball up their stories and fit them into some neatly packaged nutshell with a cursory or obligatory stamp of "faith" on it. He offered genuine insights rooted deep in his own experience, relating to them on a level others failed to achieve. His message wasn't really a "message" at all, rather a desire to honestly answer questions and be completely transparent about his belief of what sustains him in the darkest places of such an arduous trek.

He brought himself back to room 370 and Kevin. "I've rambled a bit, Kevin, and I know you're ready to go. I'm tired anyway," Dean admitted. "But I need you to know one thing."

Kevin smiled. "What's that, Mr. Moone?"

"The stories may change, but the message remains the same."

"What message?"

"Hope. Remember?" Dean asked. He turned the conversation back to where it had begun. "Hope that the *next cast* is the one to entice a trophy trout to eat your fly; hope that your double haul stands up to the wind the first time you try to fish a spring creek in Montana; hope that you have some positive impact on everyone you meet, no matter how small; hope that this," he swept his arm across his chest in a panorama of the hospital room, "isn't all there is."

Kevin's eyes met Dean's. "You know," he said softly, "I was twelve when we buried my dad. A kid that age is full of questions anyway, but I had *so* many. I honestly think I'd have been in juvie before I hit high school if it weren't for Uncle Jay, and his fishing."

Now Dean smiled. "So, maybe fly fishing saved us both."

"Maybe."

Chapter 21

I'm ready for the winds to change,
I'm ready for a brighter day.

Mac Powell, Third Day, I'm Ready

While Dean and Kevin talked faith and fly fishing, Krista meanwhile focused every last strand of energy and concentration into following the instructions she received from the staff. By mid-afternoon on Saturday, they all gave Dean and Krista a send off, and just like that, the couple found themselves back in Marietta.

They made their way into the house and tried to settle in as best they could. Everything went reasonably well until evening, when they made their way upstairs for bed. Krista busied herself with last minute preparations for the next day when she heard a loud thud. Her heart sank. A moan immediately followed. She raced through the den to the stairs.

Dean lay sprawled across the lower flight.

"Dean!" Krista gasped.

Pain seared through Dean's right arm, and he couldn't move. "I'm okay, hon," he responded. "I just can't get up. My legs are spaghetti. I couldn't lift them up to get to the next step. And now, I can't pull myself up either. I'm so sorry," he paused. "You're gonna have to call

Alan."

Krista trembled, from adrenaline, not fear. She possessed an iron will stronger than any man Dean had ever known, and he knew he was in better hands with her than anywhere else on the planet in that moment.

Her hand rested on his back. "You're sure you're not hurt?"

"No," he lied. "Really, it's okay."

Krista rushed to the phone and dialed Alan Lee's number from memory. He and Lacey had lived next door for over a decade, and had been faithful friends throughout Dean's illness.

Alan noticed the number on the Caller ID and picked up on the first ring. "Krista?"

"Alan!" she said. "Thank goodness. I need help. Dean fell going up the stairs. He says he's not hurt, but I can't lift him alone. He's too weak to get up."

"On my way," came the reply. "Sit tight."

Krista opened the front door on her way back to the stairs so Al could come straight in without ringing the bell. She sat next to Dean on the stair, holding his hand. "Al's on his way," she said.

"Krista, I'm sorry."

"Don't start," she said firmly. "I don't imagine you did this on purpose, so I don't need an apology." She rested her head on the spindle of the banister. "And," she went on, "if this is about anything else than you being spread-eagle on our stairs at this specific moment, I can't handle it. So, *don't start*. Let's just wait for Al."

As if on cue, they heard the call from the front door. "Hey y'all!"

"On the stairs!" Krista yelled.

Krista saw that Lacey tagged closely behind Al, nodding to her as she lined up along Dean's right side while Al settled on the left. Al had asked his wife, a nurse, to come, thinking Krista would draw comfort from her presence. They hoisted Dean upright, and not only settled him upstairs but stayed until Krista got all the meds taken care of and ready for the next day.

"I don't know how to thank you," Krista said as she walked the neighbors to the door.

"We wouldn't have been anywhere else," Al replied. "You know we're only a phone call away if you need *anything*."

Sunday proved fairly uneventful, with Krista busying herself with her new nursing role, and Dean so exhausted and nauseated that the whole day ebbed and flowed in a numbing routine. Then, Monday night, again as Dean went up the stairs, he let out a yell. He and Krista managed to make it up the stairs, but this time there was no hiding the fact Dean's pain was excruciating.

The visit at the clinic the next day revealed just what had happened. Dean had torn a muscle in two places, simply by holding onto the stair-rail, trying to pul himself up the stairs. The root of the main problem, they explained, stemmed from the two steroids he was taking to fight the GVHD.

"Unfortunately," the doctor explained to Krista, "the steroids cause his muscles to atrophy. My suspicion is that he can walk on flat surfaces, but lifting his legs will be almost impossible." The doctor turned to Dean, "I wouldn't use the stairs anymore if you can avoid it."

After they returned from the clinic, Krista helped Dean move to his office on the main floor. Just as he had designed it from the beginning, Dean's beautiful office and full bath provided a haven from the current storm. Built to look like a log cabin, holding fishing memories with photos that froze happier moments, the room served his needs well. Being there allowed him to come and go from the house without using any steps, and alleviated at least *some* emotional worry for Krista.

The next few days, however, brought one challenge after another. The pumps and bags with meds weighed between fifteen and twenty pounds when full, and simply getting from one place to another exhausted Dean. While being in his office eased some of the problems, he continued to weaken, and the situation quickly unraveled.

Meanwhile, Krista juggled work responsibilities and caring for Dean. A steady stream of caregivers—"babysitters" Dean called them—tried to maintain the status quo during the day. But it took Krista nearly an hour, twice a day, to prepare the nutrition bag, and when Dean tore the muscle in his chest going up the stairs it greatly limited the use of his right arm. In less than a week, they'd both had enough.

Dean looked over at Krista. She perched herself on the arm of his favorite recliner, attempting to act uninterested in the day's mail, while Dean stretched out on the couch.

"Hey hon," he said.

"Hmmm?"

"I'm really glad to be home, but," he took in a slow, deep breath, "I don't think I can do this another day."

She looked up from a Belk sales flyer. "What are you saying, Dean?"

"Something I didn't think you'd ever hear me say…I want to ask Dr. Richards if we can go back to the hospital."

Stunned silence, then, "Are you sure this is what you want to do?" she asked.

"Honey, *look* at us," Dean replied. "We're both completely exhausted. You're trying to do things six normal people can't even do. I know you've got to be feeling as overwhelmed as I am."

She nodded as tears started their run down her smooth cheeks. Krista felt there must be permanent grooves in them by now, like the way ski slopes are visible during the summer. "You're right. I *am* exhausted. And I've been even more worried about you being here, whether the care you're getting is really adequate. I spend every day a nervous wreck."

Dean's cheeks glistened with the same raw emotion as Krista's. "What have I done to you?" he choked. "Oh baby, I wish I could make all this go away."

Krista's head jerked up quickly and then back down. "Humph," she said. "Don't you think I know that?" She pushed herself from the chair and knelt by the couch. "I'd trade places with you in a split second if it would spare you one minute of this pain," she said, laying her head on his shoulder.

He leaned his head to touch hers. "This is all something, huh? We can't do this anymore, Krista."

She looked up at him, eyes softening. She felt utterly helpless. The man she'd loved since their third date now wasted away before her eyes, and she knew she'd do anything in her power to help him. "I'll call the doctor if you're really sure."

"I just can't do this anymore. Not here."

In less than an hour, the couple arrived back at the Bone Marrow Unit at Northside Hospital. The next morning, following his first decent night of sleep in over a week, Dean felt well enough to fire up his laptop for one of his famous "health updates." He brought his many friends and prayer warriors up to speed on how he'd come to arrive back at Northside, and even managed to maintain his normal sense of humor:

From this point, my guess is that we'll be on a day-to-day basis to see where we stand, and I am still eating some solid food each day which is one of the keys to my recovery. I'm probably up to 3 or 4 spoonfuls a day now. Sometimes it goes well, creating very little pain, and sometimes it doesn't go so well. It will be a very long, slow road back to providing enough nutrition on my own. I am still retaining between 20 and 25 pounds of fluid, which doesn't help my mobility one bit. A little pudgy to say the least. But it's a net gain thing, as we're estimating I've lost about 70 'real' pounds.

So, now I am back with my mistress, Queen Pole von Pumps-and-Bags, in the hospital where I really should be, and back to working hard to get well. I believe I am starting physical therapy tomorrow. Sounds fitting for Labor Day. Good news is that as of last Friday, I finished my last round of one of the steroids which should allow me to start getting some of my strength back.

I am still very confident, that with God's mercy and grace, along with your prayers and support, we will beat this disease. Specifically, please pray for my perseverance, for these torn muscles to heal quickly, and for my ability to eat more and more solid food each day without some of the severe side effects that sometimes goes along with that.

I love you all, and I still need you more than ever. Thank you for hanging in for so long. May God bless you abundantly.

With love,

Dean

Chapter 22

With rivers as with good friends,
you always feel better for a few hours
in the their presence;
you always want to review your dialogue,
years later,
with a particular pool or riffle or bend,
and to live back through layers of experience.
We have been to this river before
and together we have so much to relive.

Nick Lyons, Bright Rivers

Jimmy was exasperated, and it showed. "I just don't understand how you can be so flippin' joyous in the middle of all this. Honestly, it's a little intimidating. Not to mention annoying."

Dean looked surprised. "Oh, well, so sorry. Didn't realize my cancer was so emotionally inconvenient for you. You could be like a whole lot of other people and just quit calling or coming by. I'm sure that would be much easier for you." Now Dean was the one who was exasperated.

"I didn't mean it that way and you know it," answered Jimmy.

"Do I?" Dean sounded defeated. "Jim, some days it's hard to

feel sure about what I know."

Jimmy's tone softened. "Look, Dean, I really didn't mean to offend you. Man, we've been buddies since junior high. Do you think I don't know you by now?"

"It's debatable when you say crap like that."

Jimmy scoffed. "I only meant it's intimidating to see how unwavering you are in your faith. It's humbling, and at the same time convicting." He paused and looked at his cuticles with nonchalance. "I'm just not so sure I could, or would, say and do the things you are if I was in the same position." He cleared his throat and then studied the laces on his sneakers. "That's all."

Dean laughed out loud. "You're talking like I'm perfect, Jimmy, which we both know I am not. Not by anybody's yardstick."

This finally made Jimmy laugh, too. He took a swig of tea and leaned back against the table in Dean and Krista's kitchen.

"Oh, just sit down, would you?" Dean poured another glass of tea and pulled out a chair at the table. He drank a few swallows at once and set the glass down on a napkin.

"Jim," he said. "It'd shock the heck out of you to know just how scared I am." Dean looked his childhood friend in the eye. "And I'd stay that way if I let myself believe for one minute that I *personally* have any control over the outcome of this whole adventure."

Jimmy leaned forward and rested his elbows on the old maple farmhouse table. He focused on a few nicks and scratches, left behind over the years as a welcome reminder of hundreds of meals with family and friends. He felt privileged to be included in that group, and didn't want it to seem any differently at this moment.

"I think I'm beginning to understand," confessed Jimmy.

"Do you? Really?" Dean wasn't trying to be sarcastic, rather was yearning for this understanding from his dear friend. He desperately needed to know that someone could identify with everything he was feeling. "Jim, it's all so simple when I break it down. I could try to overanalyze it but it wouldn't make a difference."

"And what is that?" Jimmy asked.

"It really comes down to faith. I don't want to have cancer. I don't want to put Krista or Maggie through this. Again. Quite frankly, I don't want to be put through this. But if I don't believe it's for a reason, a greater purpose, where is the hope?"

Dean went on, not offering a chance for Jimmy to comment. "If God gave us a choice, do you really think we'd ever *ask* to suffer? I don't think I'd get down on my knees and pray for struggles and tests of faith to come our way. But I have to believe HE knows what the outcome is. He knows what opportunities and gifts lie within this experience."

Dean was on a roll now and did not stop. "Who am *I*, really, to doubt that? To doubt Him? No, I'm not perfect, and my faith is far from perfect. But my God is. And so is His love. To put stock in anything else totally dismisses everything I've always said I believed. After everything I've been through in the last twenty years, I cannot and will not believe that God has turned His back on me; consequently, it'd be ridiculous to think I could turn my faith away from Him."

Dean didn't realize he had tears running down his cheeks. All the emotion of the past few weeks had come rushing in all at once and had crested with this testimony of renewed faith.

Jimmy sat in stunned silence. He didn't know what to say, and that was truly rare coming from someone who always seemed to have the last word or some commentary to make.

"Okay," Jimmy began, shifting a little in his chair. "I can get it from a 'logic' perspective. The whole theology of it makes sense. But, I was there the first time you had to do this, and I'm watching you and your family with this all over again. I'm just not getting there as quickly from a 'heart' point of view. I'm thinking I could talk the talk, but man, you're walking the walk. It's just really cool."

Jimmy was attempting to maintain his bravado, but he knew that Dean knew him too well, so he relented and allowed his true feelings to surface, if only briefly.

"The way you're handling this is challenging me to be a better believer, and that really ticks me off about you," Jimmy finally admitted. "I'm the one who's supposed to be supporting you, and you're living out lessons of faithfulness for me."

"Pretty typical though, huh?" Dean teased. "Slacker," he added.

Jimmy laughed, and the tension began to ease in the kitchen.

"Dean?" Jimmy asked. "Don't you even get just a little angry sometimes? I mean, it's hardly fair—this whole thing."

"At first," Dean admitted in total candor. "I'm not sure how you can get the news I got and *not* be angry, at least for a while…Shocked. Disappointed. You name it…my emotions ran the full gamut."

Jimmy just nodded, and allowed Dean to continue with his thoughts.

"I've never felt so helpless, you know, being the control freak that I am," Dean snickered a little. "But somehow, Jim, in a way I can't explain, I arrived at this feeling of complete peace. I just truly believe in my deepest heart that God is in control."

He paused and reached for his glass. "No matter what happens," Dean threw back the remainder of the contents and then set the glass down on the table with emphasis. "And that," he said, "means there is no downside."

He chuckled a bit, "Providing I can stay out of my own way."

Jimmy nodded in agreement and made a few comments about the impossibility of that happening, grateful all the while that his dearest friend was still his friend. And even more grateful still that he was being allowed to travel on this journey with Dean.

He'd meant what he he'd said about feeling convicted and humbled. Jimmy knew that he had already been changed by what Dean was experiencing. In his heart of hearts, he felt that part of God's purpose was already unfolding simply by strengthening the faith of others who knew Dean. Believing this, he tucked the exchange of their conversation in that special place where only the best of friends guard their shared treasures.

"I'll be there, Buddy," Jimmy whispered toward the door as he climbed in his truck. "I'll be there every step of the way."

What Jimmy didn't know was that Dean was watching as he backed out of the drive, heading back toward town. He drew in a deep breath, closing his eyes. Dean stretched, pulling his shoulder blades together and arching his neck back, side to side, then forward. He felt tired. He knew, though, that there was one more thing he had to do before he could rest.

Dean moved away from the kitchen window and rounded the corner down the hall, retreating to his office, his sanctuary. He reached for his Bible resting on the corner of the desk. The smooth coolness of the pages calmed him as he fingered through to the verses he sought. This day, Psalm 139 spoke to Dean's heart, and he began to read aloud:

Where can I go from your spirit?
Where can I flee from your presence?
If I go up to the heavens, you are there;
if I make my bed in the depths, you are there.
If I rise on the wings of the dawn,
if I settle on the far side of the sea,
even there your hand will guide me,
your right hand will hold me fast.

Dean knew God was prepared to meet him wherever he was, depth or height, and he also knew he needed to cling to that; he must remind himself God didn't require perfection, only desired relationship. *I'll do my best not to forget that You're with me through all of this.*

Chapter 23

Do not fear, for I have redeemed you;
I have called you by name, you are mine.

Isaiah 43:1

January third, Dean sat in front of his computer, shocked by the fact that an entire year had passed since his second BMT. The blessings were abundant, though they could be construed as mixed at times. On the one hand, a year had passed and he was still emailing his friends. On the other hand, a year post-transplant, Dean had planned to be back on the ponds and creeks, chasing fish with a fly rod in his hand. Yet, he remained basically confined to his home and the clinic, the progress evident, but painfully slow.

After more than four months of not eating any solid food, and losing more than seventy pounds—thanks to the graft versus host disease and the multiple viruses bombarding his fragile system—he could report he that was finally eating solid food and gaining weight. A good sign, and a huge step towards recovery. The bright spot was that he was able to cut the nutritional supplement via IV to three times a week, which provided more mobility and freedom and lifted his spirits. And though nothing he ate tasted good, at least the nausea had abated.

The weight gain promised good long-term recovery, though the times when the gains came on suddenly remained challenging. The medicines still caused him to retain fluids, and he could gain eight or ten pounds in two days. Again, Dean considered slow improvement better than none at all. Permission to drive again provided a source of new freedom, and he refused to be dampened by the fact he could only drive to the clinic and back home. The doctors told him his immune system still lacked the punch to fight off infections, especially during flu season.

He ticked out an email to his loyal and faithful friends, remaining amazed and humbled by the number of people who continued to stick by him and his family. A few weeks before Christmas, a group of friends had come and split firewood for the house. Before that, one friend had come to get Dean's car to take it for a detail, while another group had stayed at the house, raking leaves, mulching flower beds, painting some shutters, and dragging limbs to the curb. He constantly wondered how he would ever be able to adequately thank them for all they'd done.

Once the email was sent, Dean leaned back in his chair. Many times along this second journey, he'd found solace seated in the worn leather, feeling the strong oak of his father's old desk. It kept him grounded, connected. He glanced at the wall to pictures of past fishing trips. Smiling faces and trophy trout beckoned him to return to them. He knew that his final affirmation of beating this horrible disease a second time would be the day he cast a line. It frustrated him to sit on his butt and wonder when that day would indeed come.

Dean realized he had come off the heels of a very frustrating

Christmas season. Normally, with Krista out of school for holiday break, they were able to do many things together. Past breaks brought roaring fires Dean built in their stone fireplace, movies and dinners out with friends, short trips up to the mountain cabin. The prior year, the joke among them had been "chemo for Christmas and a bone marrow transplant for New Year's Eve." He and Krista had both prepared themselves for that season, and seemed to not be as affected by it all.

Then, they had spent their anniversary at the hospital. Each time they seemed to make a little progress, a caveat or limiting factor entered the mix. So, during this Christmas season, Dean had fought the depression that tried to creep in. True to form, God always seemed to step in at just the right time.

Dean and Krista sat in front of the fire, feet propped up, each engrossed in a book. Dean plopped his book on his lap and looked at his wife.

"Do you hear something?" he asked.

"Like what?"

"I'm honestly not sure," he said, "it almost sounds like... singing."

Krista pushed herself from the couch and went toward the front windows of their home. She realized it was, in fact, singing. As she pulled back the curtains, her eyes filled with tears.

"Dean!" she called. "You need to come see this."

As Dean came up behind his wife, his jaw dropped. Standing in front of his house were a dozen members of their Sunday School class, wrapped in coats and singing carols. They had known that Dean would be unable to attend Advent or Christmas Eve services, and how much he loved music. As a group, they decided to instead bring the music to Dean.

"*O come all ye faithful, joyful and triumphant...*" sailed across the air as Dean and Krista opened the front door to listen. After five or six of Dean's favorite hymns, he and his wife were heartbroken not to be able to invite everyone in, but they knew the group understood. The friends departed, calling over their shoulders and promising to return for visits soon. When the couple closed the door, they stood in silence, wrapped in each other's embrace, thankful for the blessings of the season.

"Merry Christmas," Krista whispered.

"Merry Christmas."

Chapter 24

I was there to hear your borning cry,
I'll be there when you are old.

John Ylvisaker, *Borning Cry*

Sixteen months after Dean's second bone marrow transplant, he waited at his dining room table for Krista and Maggie to re-enter the room, his eyes closed tightly because they had made him swear not to peek until they returned. Tonight, they celebrated Dean's birthday. For Dean, unlike many past dates marking the anniversary of his birth, this particular night felt right for celebration. He *wanted* the fanfare, and he wanted to devour too much of the cake, and he loved making a really big deal about a calendar entry. In so many ways, this birthday symbolized everything Dean had prayed would come to fruition.

As he sat lost in his own thoughts, his wife and daughter re-entered the room.

"Hey!" Maggie barked playfully, "No peeking!"

Dean held up his hands like a criminal under arrest. "I'm trying to be good, I promise."

They all laughed and Krista and Maggie seated themselves on

either side of Dean.

"Okay," said Krista, "open your eyes!"

Spread before him sat several boxes, of various sizes. Typical birthdays in the Moone household usually brought a card or maybe a dinner out; once Maggie passed the age of around twelve, the large celebrations fizzled out. This took Dean by surprise.

"Wow," he exclaimed. "So, what do I open first?"

Maggie reached for a smallish box and pushed it toward Dean. "Here," she said, "open this one."

Dean tore off the paper and carefully opened the box. A five-by-seven frame held an enlarged snapshot of Maggie holding her first trout. She giggled at the look on her dad's face, and Dean beamed.

"Very cool, Bugs," he said, obviously touched. "What a great gift. I still remember that like it was yesterday."

Two more boxes came. A fly fishing book he'd been wanting, a new pocketknife. One box was from his Sunday School class. "Wonder what this is?" he said.

He opened the box and found a letter from one of his friends in the class. Seemed they all made calls and sent some emails, and bottom line was, when he felt well enough and got the doctor's release, a trout-fishing trip to Montana awaited him, all expenses paid. In addition to the letter, the box contained pictures and pamphlets about the lodge where they would stay and the fishing they would encounter.

"Oh man!" Dean said. "You've gotta be *kidding* me! This is unbelievable!"

Then, Krista shoved the largest box toward Dean. It measured about two feet in height and almost three feet across, and took up most of the end of their dining table. When he picked it up, he found it to be surprisingly light. He pulled off the top and stared down. Three cards lay inside with brightly colored paper underneath. He saw one card was from Sam, one from Jimmy and the other from Krista. He opened them one by one and was already close to tears when Krista prompted him to remove the colored paper.

"What?" he asked.

"The paper," she said, throwing up her hands, "take out the paper."

As soon as Dean removed the colored paper, he started to cry. Not just a few tears of happiness, but a flood of jubilation. "What on earth," he said, wiping his eyes, "is all this?"

Beneath the three cards and other paper, Dean found the *entire box* filled with cards. Unbeknownst to him, for weeks Krista had been intercepting and gathering cards sent from multitudes of supporters. A single email from her a couple months before his birthday, sent to his entire "update" email list, prompted an unexpected and overwhelming response. Cards flooded the mailbox over the following weeks, with Krista stowing them away until the big day. From what Dean could gather, there were now before his eyes several hundred cards. He was speechless.

It took most of the week, but Dean read every single card. What shocked him the most were the cards in which the inscription began, "We've never met, but so-and-so has been forwarding me your emails for months." Others mentioned meeting only once or twice, but that the sender had been praying for Dean's recovery. The most precious gifts, he concluded, were the unexpected ones, the ones that could never even be imagined.

"You're *amazing*. Do you know that?" Dean asked Krista over dinner one night later that week.

"Hmmm?" she mused.

"First of all, you come up with this whole idea about people sending the cards," he explained, "then, you run yourself crazy, sneaking the mail in and keeping it all a big secret, then spring all this on me." He smiled, then looked down at the floor. "I just know I haven't told you enough during all this how much I appreciate you."

"Now don't go all mushy on me," she teased. "It's *so* not your style."

He reached out and stroked her cheek with the back of his fingers. Those cheeks had harbored thousands of tears in the last couple of years. *Too many*. And yet, this incredible woman had stuck by him every step of the way, even when he tried to run her off.

"Krista," he said, his voice low and hoarse, "I mean it. All of this is so unexpected. I just am overwhelmed, and have no idea how to express to you what it means to be married to you, to have your love and support. Where would I be right now without it?"

She smiled, taking his hand from her cheek and holding it in hers. "Lucky for me," she said, kissing his fingers, "neither of us ever have to find out. If you haven't figured it out by now, you're stuck with me."

"Thank God," he said. And he meant it with every fiber of his being. "No matter what the doctor has in store for us tomorrow," he added, "this birthday will be hard to top."

When they arrived at the doctor's office, their wait was short and soon a nurse ushered them into the examining room to wait for the doctor. In less than ten minutes, Dr. Richards rapped quickly on the door and entered in usual fashion.

"Ah, Dean," he greeted, "good to see you!"

"Likewise," Dean responded.

The doctor reviewed Dean's chart, taking in the results of the latest tests. He closed the folder and took off his glasses.

"Dean," he began, "it appears to me I've missed one very crucial item in your file."

Dean tensed and braced himself for yet another round of bad news. At this point, nothing surprised him anymore.

"I think," the doctor smiled, "that I missed your birthday!"

Dean jerked back in his chair, glancing from the doctor to his wife.

"Excuse me?" he said.

"Well," said the doctor, "in all of recent scans and test-running, your birthday snuck up on me, and I couldn't let it pass without giving you *my* present."

"O…kaaay."

Dr. Richards handed Dean a single sheet of paper. Dean scanned it and looked up at the doctor with a start, his eyes big and wide. "Is this really *true*?" he asked. "You're really serious?"

The doctor nodded, his expression grim. "Yes, Dean," he said, "I'm afraid so. That's the latest of the results, and they're very accurate."

Dean let the paper fall to the floor and put his face in his hands. He sat like that for several minutes and no one in the room said a word.

Then, without warning, he jumped up, grabbing Krista and kissing her full on the lips.

"We did it!" he yelled. "HE did it! Oh, thank you, *thank you.*"

Krista stood stunned, anxious for an explanation. She looked from Dean to Dr. Richards and back again. "Someone want to let me in on what was on that paper?"

Dean spun on his heel to face his wife again. "We…are…done! *Done*—do you hear?"

"What?"

Dr. Richards spoke up, "Yes, that's right. All of the blood work is where I'd like it to be. The latest scans are negative. By Dean's yardstick, and thereby maybe the most important result of all….he can go fishing."

Krista's eyes brimmed immediately.

"Happy Birthday, Dean," said the doctor. "Just use your brain with the fishing thing, okay? We'll still be doing scans and bloodwork every eight weeks for the next six months or so."

"Doctor," Dean said, "you could tether me to a tree if you want, as long as I get to wade in a creek and feel the tug on the end of a fly line!"

"Have at it, man," said the doctor. "And catch one for me."

The Epilogue to this story is indeed fiction. Dean Moone, or at least the man whose story is woven into Dean's life, is still very much alive and well. His message and life represent hope, for all of us, and a determined faith that doesn't demand immediate answers or perpetual sunshine to endure.

In that light, I sensed readers might imagine their own "ending" for Dean's journey. If that is the case for you, then please, read no further and pass the book to a friend. For others who hunger for closure, the next chapters offer my hope for what God has in store for my dear friend. As readers ease back into Dean's life, much later, they find Maggie grown, now with a family of her own. And, as usual, someone is fishing....

Epilogue

All their life in this world and all their
adventures in Narnia
had only been the cover and the title page:
now at last they were beginning
Chapter One of the Great Story
which no one on earth has read:
which goes on forever:
in which every chapter is better
than the one before.

C.S. Lewis, The Last Battle

Dean absolutely loved fishing with his granddaughter. Claire's new job made the gaps between their outings longer and longer, and Dean selfishly looked forward to having these times with just the two of them. With another promotion for her looming on the horizon, Dean sensed that this trend would only continue, and given that he was still in good health (for ninety-four anyway), he wasn't going to let anything stand in the way of another fabulous weekend.

His memory drifted to fishing times like this with Claire's mother, his Maggie, his Buga Bear. So many months and years passed during her childhood when he questioned whether he would see her get married, or achieve so many of the milestones he had been privileged to share in her life. Now, his granddaughter was grown and on her own! For Dean, the passing of time was the biggest blessing of all.

Coming to the cabin this weekend had been a treat they both needed, and each had enjoyed it immensely for their own reasons. As they made their way up the winding gravel drive, the cabin beckoned them closer, nestled in the tall swaying pines. The front porch swing still had the same red and white gingham pillows tossed on either end, and the two rockers stood waiting at attention for their company, like saddled horses grazing while waiting for their riders.

They shared morning coffee on the porch, as they'd arrived very early—even for them. They made their plans for where they would fish, and at what times of the day, before loading their vests and heading down to the creek.

This day had been particularly special, one of those days when it seemed everything was just as it all should be in the world. They'd spent a good part of the first half of the day at their favorite fishing hole, catching what they both thought were some really nice trout. The water was quick and clear, and the slightly overcast skies made for some fine midge fishing.

What Dean loved about midge fishing was something that paralleled his Christian life. Midges follow a life cycle similar to caddisflies, with a larval, pupal, and adult stage; while all three are important to the trout he loved to catch, the pupal was the most important because it drifts in the current. As a follower of Christ, Dean loved the analogy that you didn't have to be all grown up and perfect in your faith to be useful and meaningful to others. What makes midges such an important trout food despite their size is the fact that they hatch all year long, so they may be the only source of easy food in a trout stream in the middle of winter. This, too, Dean loved matching to his faith. Even though he was only one man, he could still do great things, even in the midst of his own personal "winters"—such as the trials he had survived with the two BMTs.

They'd tied on double flies, with a size 22 midge below an 18 Copper John, about 18 inches apart. While Dean had laughed during many a heated debate about strike indicator use, he had concluded after getting skunked numerous times that midge fishing without indicators was like using a bare hook to try to catch a catfish. Oh, sure, it could be done, but it took a lot longer, was pretty frustrating, and didn't really seem to require more fishing skill than using bait. At ninety-four, Dean had decided that the thrill of catch-and-release outweighed the thrill of maybe outsmarting one trout without an indicator on any given day. If he'd been completely honest, the other reason was at his age he simply couldn't see the line as well anymore and missed a lot of fish without the indicator. Dean and Claire worked in tandem, as they had so many times; working about 20 yards or so apart, they followed a choreographed river dance of sorts, casting to the head of the run, dead-drifting its full length, and watching the strike indicator swing out of the current before lifting the line to cast again.

An occasional yelp of "Fish on!" broke the silence.

To truly grasp the joy that mornings like these held for them requires an understanding of the connection of the sport and, in turn, how the sport connected them to each other. It was the tug of the current around their calves as they waded, the cool splash of a released fish. In their quiet togetherness, Dean had taught Claire to listen for what God might say to her in the bubbling of the water.

As they repeated this series over and over, each would move upstream a couple of steps every third or fourth cast, enabling them to cover more water and have a crack at more trout.

Dean always put Claire upstream of himself, giving her first pass at the wary fish, and they could fish for over an hour without much conversation. Both were content to enjoy the gentle pressure of the water against their legs as they waded along, taking in the gurgling of the water over the rocks and the sounds coming from the surrounding woods.

Each time they stole away a Saturday at the cabin, the pair topped off the morning's fishing with a lunch on the banks of the creek. Claire brought their standard special lunch—sliced jalapeno-jack cheese, carved smoked turkey, grape tomatoes, olives, and Triscuits. Of course, they always washed it down with Diet Coke, and spent nearly as much time gabbing and laughing as they did eating.

On this particular day, while they polished off another streamside buffet, Dean moved closer to Claire.

"Ok, Sugar Snap," Dean winked, "here's the deal..."

"What are you talking about, D?" Claire tried to act gruff, but the truth was she loved that her grandfather still used his pet name for her, even after all these years. She was, however, puzzled all the same.

Dean pulled a set of papers from his fishing vest and thrust them at the granddaughter who had become his best fishing buddy after Jimmy died over a decade before. Though she had blossomed into a beautiful woman at almost thirty-eight, Dean still saw her as the red-haired freckle-faced angel who first fished with him in these waters over thirty years earlier. In so many ways, the times spent fishing with Claire mirrored times spent with the other favorite redhead in his life, his daughter Maggie. He felt so proud, so happy that they both shared his passion for fly fishing. The decision he had made, the one he was now sharing, had come so easily.

Claire reached out, a puzzled look on her face, and took the papers from her grandfather. She really had no idea what they were, and put them on her lap without opening them.

"What's up, D?" she asked.

"Why don't you just look at the darn papers and find out for yourself?" he replied. "It's not a snake you know."

Claire laughed nervously at her grandfather's choice of words. She hated snakes, and he knew it. He still remembered the time she had shinned up the support post of the front porch—faster than any squirrel—after she had nearly stepped on a copperhead sunning on the path. He stifled a snicker at the memory, willing himself back to the present.

"Claire, why don't you just look them over," he urged again, more gently now. She carefully unfolded the document, and had to scan down a few paragraphs before she realized what it was. Her eyes opened wide about half way down the second page, and were filling with tears by the time she looked at Dean.

"Oh, D! Are you really sure about this?" She could hardly believe the blessing of it all. Her grandfather had deeded the cabin to Claire; it was now hers, lock, stock and barrel. She had hoped for this, but not dared dream it would actually happen. It was her "connected" place—the one place in the world she could feel so in tune with her own thoughts and her faith. This happening today was the answer to a prayer. The fact that Dean had wanted it to be this way made it all the more special.

He put his arm around her, tugging her toward him, grinning. "Do you really think I could ever leave this place to anyone but you, Sugar Snap?"

She snapped out of her reverie, sniffling, and laid her head on his shoulder. Dean continued, "You're the only one who gets as much joy out of this place as I do, Claire. This way, I know it'll always be in good hands."

"I promise to always take good care of it, D," she said. "I just had a thought—why don't I go get some of those good, gooey cookies, and we can celebrate a *perfect* day?"

Dean pushed himself up from the old log that doubled as their bench, brushing off his pants legs, and moved over by the hammock. "You know, Snap," he said yawning, "you take your time getting all the other stuff together." Lifting his legs over the edge of the hammock, he continued, "I think I'm just gonna stretch out here for a bit; all this excitement's worn me out. Oh, and catching a few more fish than my granddaughter!" He giggled, and pulled his cap down over his eyes a bit after he'd settled himself fully in the hammock, and Claire turned to make her way back up the hill toward the cabin.

After about forty-five minutes or so, Claire glanced at the antique clock on the wall, and figured they had better be heading back toward civilization before all the other sticks in the mud worried about them. It had been such a great day, full of so many blessings, that she hated to leave; at least she knew there would be many more now that Dean had given her the cabin. She decided she'd load everything in the truck first, and give her grandfather a few more minutes to cat nap in the hammock before waking him.

Another fifteen minutes or so later, Claire made her way back down the path to the creekside hammock to wake her grandfather.

"Hey, D!" she called down the hill. "Better get a move on—Grana will have a search party out for us if we're not back before dark." Claire kept walking as she spoke, her words keeping a sort of rhythm with the crunching of the pea gravel under her feet.

Dean didn't answer right away, but Claire wasn't really surprised; his hearing had worsened with age, and he definitely could always sleep through a tornado even in his younger days! Claire walked on to the hammock and gently shook Dean's shoulder as she lifted his cap.

"D," she roused, "we gotta go. C'mon, you're not that old yet." Then, as if someone had hit her in the stomach, Claire realized what had happened. He was gone. She crumpled to her knees beside the hammock, the pine needles pricking through her pants. Her arms folded across her stomach as she rocked herself back and forth under the pines, weeping.

Dean's face looked so peaceful, and she couldn't help but think he looked almost happy. She knew what a devoted Christian her grandfather was, and was always envious of the deep personal relationship he had with the Lord. Still, Claire couldn't help but feel very sad that she'd just lost her best fishing pal and spiritual advisor. She knew that the rest of the family would be devastated, and probably even chide her a bit for letting Dean talk her into going fishing so often.

Nevertheless, Claire knew in her heart of hearts that her grandfather had left this world on his own terms, and would now be able to live forever with God.

She had no doubt about the existence of heaven. Dean had told her many times about his experience when he was about the age she was now; of the clearing where God had told him it was not yet his time, of the peace and complete lack of fear he had about the entire concept of death. Now it really *was* his time, and she had been blessed to spend his last hours with him, doing the things they both loved to do.

Claire pulled herself back to the moment, knowing she needed to inform the others of what had happened. Reaching into her pocket, she called her mother on her cell phone. Claire related the details of the day, and asked her mom to meet her at Grana's house. She'd have to call the proper authorities and be sure everything was taken care of, and then she could meet her family at her grandmother's house. As the devoted granddaughter took care of all the details in silent tears, she did so unaware that her beloved "D" had started his next journey…

o o o o o

Dean found himself back in a clearing, and knew right where he was this time and recognized every tree. The songs of the birds were even more joyful and splendid than they had been the first time, and he felt perfect peace. He realized now, different from the first time, that when he heard voices he also saw people. But, before he could say anything to anyone else, the light gained intensity, and he heard a familiar voice.

Welcome home, Dean.

"Am I here for good this time?"

The leaves danced their familiar dance in the swirling wind.

Yes, you're home for good. And we're all so full of joy. There are a lot of people waiting to see you.

And so there were. His mother was there, with her dancing blue eyes and musical laugh. She looked to be only about in her mid-forties, but still looked like herself. She hugged and kissed him, weeping tears of joy. She called to others, announcing Dean's arrival, and people began coming from all over the wood. He hugged his brother, Jimmy, and Sam, and they all laughed and talked—for how long Dean did not know. It didn't matter that one lost track of time, because it seemed that time passed differently now.

Presently, a path became visible on the other side of the clearing. Dean felt drawn to follow the path, and found that it led to a stream.

Not any ordinary stream; it was the most magnificent stream he could have imagined in any of his wildest dreams. He'd never seen water that color; a blend of shimmering silver, deep blue, emerald green, swirling and dancing over boulders as smooth as glass. Overhead, eagles and hawks soared together, playing winged games of tag and trumpeting welcomes to the new resident of the Valley. Dean knew at that moment he could have never imagined heaven if he'd lived another ninety-four years. Or one hundred and ninety-four.

He dipped some of the water from the stream and splashed it on his face. It was cool, soothing, and seemed to wash a perfect peace over his entire soul. He looked down at his hands and noticed they were no longer the sun-spotted, wrinkled hands that had tied midges on fly line earlier that day, but they were the hands of his youth. His body was young, strong, and free of all pain or infirmity.

He closed his eyes and breathed deeply, then opened them again to take in the splendor of the view. Dean knew that he would never tire of looking at it. As he glanced around, he caught the movement of a figure out of the corner of his eye. From the back, the outline was somehow warmly familiar, and he moved downstream toward it. As the figure turned to face him, Dean realized who it was. His heart leapt with joy! Waiting there for Dean, with two fly rods in his hand, stood his father.

"I've been waiting for you, Son," his father said with a smile. He held out a rod to Dean, which he took in his right hand while wiping tears of joy from his cheek with his left.

His dad continued, "There's an *outstanding* hatch going on right now—just wait'll you see what we catch *here*!"

They both laughed out loud and started casting.

"Fish on!"

The End.

Author's Note

Dean Moone's Full Circle journey is a true story. It falls in the widely accepted genre of "creative nonfiction," which is to say, there are a few things that I want you to know about the details of this book.

The events depicted here are true, representing one man's journey. Careful interviews, geographical research and technical clarifications were gathered to recreate incidents that span more than three decades. The names of the characters have been changed, but all are real people. In some instances, more than one person may be depicted as a single composite character to manage the length and flow of the story. Dialogue and inner thoughts have been recreated to match the moments as closely as possible. Some time periods have been compressed to adapt to the flow of the story; for instance, a conversation that really took place in September might take place the following March, but the content is unchanged.

I met the "real" Dean several years ago at a fly fishing fundraiser for St. Jude Children's Research Hospital. His story is compelling in and of itself, but if you ever meet him, it is his humor and his grace that captivate. When the second BMT became a reality, I approached him with the idea of this book. I admire his faith and consider it a privilege to share his story with you.

On the next page, you'll meet the real Dean and Krista Moone. Thank you for making the journey with us.

A Word from "Dean"

Full Circle is really the only appropriate title for this story... Being diagnosed with terminal cancer—not once, but twice—has turned out to be the biggest blessing of my life. Everyone will have hardships in their lives; how we deal with those hardships is, I feel, a conscious choice we make. I have chosen to let God, through my relationship with Jesus Christ, help me deal with this journey. My personal experience dictates that God has and will continue to supply everything needed to get through the hardships of life.

I firmly believe:

That only God can provide the peace and comfort we've experienced.

That only God could relieve the worries we should have had.

That with God all things are possible.

These days, virtually everyone you meet has been impacted in some way by this vicious disease. Through this journey, I have had the opportunity to speak to many people, and have witnessed how our story has touched or inspired their lives. When people find out I'm not just a survivor of cancer, but a survivor of *two terminal diagnoses*, it definitely makes an impact. I'm not just someone they read about—we've met and talked face to face. It gives them hope and inspiration. It begins, renews, or enhances their relationship with God.

I just consider it an honor that the Creator of the Universe would use me and my family in such a way.

May God bless you on your own journey,

Don Malone, aka, Dean Moone

Pictured with his wife of 31 years, *Pam, aka, Krista Moone*

Lindsay Malone,
aka, Maggie Moone

About the Author

APRIL CONRAD is a full time wife, mom and marketing executive. A graduate of Pepperdine University, she captained the women's golf team for three years before pursuing a short professional career in the sport. She currently manages local market and customer development for a Fortune 500 company.

A devoted Christian, April gives freely of her time and talents through various ministries and charitable organizations. She and her husband founded Hooked on a Cure, which supports St. Jude Children's Research Hospital through a love of fly fishing. When not pursuing her outdoor passions, April can be found cheering on her children at various little league events and activities, or working in her gardens.

Also the author of several short stories, including "The Grits Cricket," *Full Circle* is her first novel. She is currently working on her second book project. April lives in Florence, Alabama, with her husband and best friend, Will, their two amazing children, Anna and William, and a very snuggly rat terrier.

Photo by Greg Crenshaw
Crenshaw Portrait Studio, Florence, Alabama